A House Built on Lies

A House Built on Lies

A Family. A Lie. A Line You Can't Uncross.

Chiara Robbins

ISBN - Paperback: 978-1-916662-42-1
ISBN - Hardcover : 978-1-916662-41-4
ISBN - Ebook: 978-1-916662-40-7
First Edition: 2025

CONTENTS

1

THE PERFECT FACADE

Emily Johnson stared at her husband's **phone,** unable to move. The device felt heavier in her hand than it should have. The weight of her discovery seemed to add physical mass to the phone. A notification had flashed across the screen:

I can't wait to see you again. It's been too long.

She read it once more, her pulse quickening. The number wasn't saved in Mark's contacts. From the bathroom, the sound of running water provided a mundane soundtrack to her racing thoughts.

The sound of running water ceased abruptly. Mark would be out of the shower any minute. Emily placed the phone back on the coffee table exactly as she'd found it, the innocuous black rectangle now unsettling in her hand.

She settled back onto the couch, picking up the novel she'd been trying to focus on before her client meeting that afternoon. Working as a graphic designer from home had its advantages, but concentration wasn't coming easily today. She tried to slow her breathing. Her mind raced through possibilities: a colleague being overly familiar, a wrong number, or... something else. The thought that had first gripped her heart refused to release its hold.

Mark appeared in the doorway, towel-drying his hair, droplets of water still clinging to his broad shoulders. Seventeen years of marriage, and he still maintained the athletic build that had first caught her eye all those years ago. He smiled at her, unaware of the storm brewing behind her carefully composed expression.

"Find anything interesting?" he asked, nodding at her book.

"Not really." The lie came, surprisingly easily. "How was your shower?"

"Good. Hot water didn't run out, for once." He dropped onto the couch beside her, the cushions dipping under his weight. He picked up his phone and quickly swiped away the notification on the screen. His casual dismissal of the message made Emily's stomach tighten.

Was this routine for him? "Tom's been driving me crazy at work with this new project. The client wants everything yesterday, typical."

Emily nodded, watching him carefully. "Tom? Is he new?"

"I've mentioned him before. He's a financial advisor at Preston Financial. Tall guy, working with us on the Henson account?" Mark's expression remained open, relaxed. He reached for the remote, completely at ease.

"Right, of course," Emily murmured. Had he mentioned Tom before? She couldn't recall, but doubt had already taken root in her mind.

"You okay? You seem distracted." His blue eyes—the same ones that had looked at her with undisguised love on their wedding day—studied her face.

"Just tired," she said, forcing a smile. "Claire's drama with her friends is exhausting. You know how teenage girls can be."

Mark chuckled and squeezed her shoulder. "Our daughter gets her dramatic flair from your side of the family."

Emily laughed automatically, the sound hollow to her own ears. Was she being paranoid? Jumping to conclusions over a single text message? But something in her gut twisted uncomfortably, a warning she couldn't ignore.

"You've been working late a lot," she said, trying to keep her tone casual. "That big project Tom mentioned?"

Mark's shoulders stiffened almost imperceptibly. "Yeah, it's been intense. The Henderson account."

"I thought you said it was the Henson account a minute ago," Emily remarked, her heart suddenly pounding.

Mark's laugh seemed forced. "Did I? God, I'm losing my mind with all these clients." He grabbed the remote and turned on the TV, effectively ending the conversation. "Mind if I watch the game highlights?"

Emily nodded, pretending to return to her book while studying him from the corner of her eye. In seventeen years of marriage, she'd never caught Mark in a lie before—or perhaps she'd never been looking for one.

***

"You're stirring that coffee like it personally offended you."

Emily looked up to find Sarah watching her with concern. They sat at their usual corner table at Brew Haven, the café's morning rush having dwindled to a few solitary patrons tapping at laptops.

"Sorry," Emily said, setting down her spoon. "I didn't sleep well."

Sarah leaned forward, tucking a strand of chestnut hair behind her ear. "What's going on? And don't say 'nothing'—I've known you too long for that to work."

The words caught in Emily's throat. Saying them aloud would make her suspicions real, would transform her marriage into something uncertain. But Sarah had been her confidant since college, the steady presence Emily had always relied on.

"I found a text on Mark's phone yesterday," she began, her voice dropping to nearly a whisper despite the ambient chatter of the café. "From someone not in his contacts. It was..." She swallowed. "Suggestive."

Sarah's eyebrows rose. "What did it say exactly?"

"'I can't wait to see you again. It's been too long.'" Emily repeated the words that had been echoing in her mind since yesterday.

"That could be innocent," Sarah offered, but her expression had grown more serious. "A colleague, maybe?"

"That's what I told myself. But when I asked about work, he mentioned someone named Tom he's been working with closely." Emily's fingers tightened around her mug. "And then he slipped up about which client they're working with. I've never caught him in a lie before."

"Maybe he's just stressed and mixed up the names," Sarah suggested, though her tone lacked conviction. "People make mistakes when they're tired."

"It wasn't just that. He's been coming home later and later. Last week, he missed dinner three times. And there was this weird call he took in the garage at midnight—I heard him through the baby monitor we still have plugged in near Claire's old play area."

"What did he say?" Sarah's investigative reporter instincts were clearly engaged despite having left that career behind years ago.

"I couldn't make it out clearly, but he sounded angry. When I asked him about it the next morning, he said it was a wrong number. Who gets angry at a wrong number at midnight?"

"So your instincts are telling you something," Sarah said.

Emily nodded, relief washing over her at being understood. "Am I crazy for even thinking this? Mark has never given me reason to doubt him before."

Sarah reached across the table and squeezed Emily's hand. "Listen to me. Your instincts got you through your mother's illness, through Claire's difficult years in middle school, through everything life has thrown at you. Don't discount them now."

"What do I do? Confront him?"

"Not yet," Sarah said, her tone firm. "If there's something going on, you'll need more than a text message. Trust your gut, but verify with evidence. Otherwise, he'll just deny it and be more careful."

Emily felt a chill at the calculated nature of Sarah's advice, but she couldn't deny the logic. "You make it sound like I should investigate my own husband."

"If he's hiding something, Em, don't you want to know what it is?" Sarah's eyes held hers steadily. "For your sake and for Claire's?"

Emily thought of her sixteen-year-old daughter, blissfully unaware of the doubt that had crept into their perfect suburban life. Claire, who had Mark's blue eyes and Emily's stubborn determination. Who deserved better than a foundation built on lies.

"Yes," Emily said finally, resolve hardening within her. "I need to know the truth."

The coffee between them had grown cold, forgotten in the weight of the moment. Outside, clouds gathered on the horizon, casting shadows across the café's large windows.

While they were leaving, Emily noticed their neighbor Frank Peterson watching them from across the street. He quickly averted his gaze when she noticed. Strange—she hadn't spoken to Frank in months. Was he always this interested in her comings and goings?

"Do you know Frank Peterson well?" Emily asked Sarah, nodding discreetly in his direction.

Sarah glanced over. "Not really. He's on the neighborhood watch committee with Lisa Turner and a few others. Why?"

"No reason," Emily said, dismissing the thought. She had bigger concerns than nosy neighbors right now.

2

SECRETS IN THE SHADOWS

Emily waited until Mark left for an "early meeting" before beginning her search. His kiss on her cheek had felt perfunctory this morning, lacking the warmth she once took for granted. Had it been that way for months now? She couldn't pinpoint when the shift had occurred.

"I'll be late tonight," he'd told her at breakfast, not quite meeting her eyes. "Another dinner with the Henderson team."

"The Henderson account again?" Emily had asked carefully, watching his reaction.

"Yeah. Big client. Lots of moving parts." Mark had smiled, but it didn't reach his eyes. "Don't wait up."

She'd nodded and waved him goodbye, maintaining the façade of normalcy while her mind raced with questions. Now, with Mark safely out of the house, she could search for answers.

She moved methodically through their living room, starting with the side table where Mark often tossed his keys and wallet. Nothing unusual. The bookshelf didn't yield anything either, though she noted with a pang that the travel guides they'd bought for their tenth-anniversary trip to Italy were gathering dust. They'd talked about returning for their twentieth, but lately, Mark changed the subject whenever vacation plans came up.

Emily hesitated at Mark's desk drawer. In twelve years of sharing this house, she'd never felt the need to rifle through his belongings. Perhaps she was the betrayer here, she realized, invading his privacy, assuming the worst. When had mistrust replaced the faith they once shared?

When did we become strangers? she wondered, sliding the drawer open.

Inside his work diary was a printed photograph of his entire team. She recognized everyone but one face. A man, sitting next to Mark, wearing a smirk on his face that didn't quite reach his eyes. *This must be Tom*, she realized.

Pens, paperclips, and a half-empty pack of gum. She was about to close the drawer when her fingers brushed against something tucked in the back. A plain manila envelope, unlabeled and sealed with a small metal clasp.

Her hands trembled slightly as she opened it. Inside were several receipts, neatly preserved as if for tax purposes. Her stomach tightened as she examined them: a charge for $340 at Vespri's, the upscale Italian restaurant; a hotel bill from The Westbrook for a "business accommodation"; and three separate bar tabs from places she'd never heard of, all with dates from the past two months.

Beneath the receipts, Emily found something that made her blood run cold—a small silver key with an unfamiliar logo and a numbered tag: "Storage Unit #47." She turned it over in her palm, wondering what Mark could possibly need to keep in a storage unit she'd never heard of.

Further digging revealed a small notebook with columns of numbers and initials. The figures were substantial—some in the tens of thousands. Next to one entry marked "JM –45K" was a small check mark and the notation "cleaned." The business jargon seemed suspicious. What legitimate transaction needed to be "cleaned"?

A movement outside caught her eye. Through the bay window, she saw Lisa Turner kneeling in her front garden across the street, her attention suspiciously fixed on Emily's house rather than the tulips she was supposedly tending. When their eyes met, Lisa quickly looked away, suddenly absorbed in her gardening.

That's odd, Emily thought. But Lisa wasn't the only one

acting strange lately. Just yesterday, she'd noticed Frank Peterson walking his dog past their house three times in a single hour. And the new couple at the end of the block—the Millers—had invited them to dinner with unusual persistence.

Or perhaps finding evidence of my husband's secret affair is just making me paranoid.

Affair.

Could it be true?

Or was it something worse? These receipts, the storage unit key, the notebook with large sums of money... This didn't feel like just an affair anymore.

Emily returned her focus to the receipts. The dates corresponded with evenings when Mark claimed to be working late or having drinks with colleagues. Her mind drifted to four weeks ago, when he'd come home after midnight smelling faintly of unfamiliar cologne, claiming the scent must have transferred from a client he'd met earlier. She'd believed him then. She felt so naïve.

She slipped the receipts and the key into her pocket and replaced the envelope exactly as she'd found it. The notebook was too risky to take—Mark might notice its absence—so she quickly photographed several pages with her phone instead. Evidence gathered, but at what cost?

***

"You look like you've seen a ghost," Sarah said, closing Emily's front door behind her. She carried two take-out coffees from Brew Haven, a small gesture of normality in what had become Emily's increasingly surreal existence.

"Maybe I have," Emily replied, leading her friend to the kitchen. The afternoon sun streamed through the windows, casting patterns on the granite countertop where they'd shared countless conversations over the years. "The ghost of my marriage."

Sarah's expression shifted from concern to alarm. "What happened?"

Emily pulled the receipts from her pocket and spread them on the counter like playing cards in a losing hand. "I found these hidden in Mark's desk."

She placed the storage unit key beside them. "And this. He's never mentioned having a storage unit." She unlocked her phone and showed Sarah the photos of the notebook. "Plus this... it looks like some kind of accounting ledger, but none of it makes sense. These amounts are huge."

Sarah examined them carefully, her brow furrowing. "These dates—you were home alone on these nights?"

"Yes. Working late, client dinners, industry events— that's what he told me." Emily wrapped her arms around herself, suddenly cold despite the warm spring day. "I remembered something else, too. Last Christmas party at his firm, I overheard his colleague Jeff asking about 'the cabin weekend.' Mark cut him off quickly, said it was canceled.

He never mentioned any cabin weekend to me."

"These don't look like normal business expenses," Sarah said, studying the notebook figures. "And what does 'cleaned' mean next to this amount?"

"I don't know, but it sounds... illegal? Could Mark be involved in something criminal?"

Sarah's expression grew grave. "I hate to say it, but this looks more serious than an affair, Em. These kinds of records, the secret storage unit... it reminds me of those money laundering cases I covered when I was still reporting for the *Tribune*."

"You think he's..." Sarah didn't finish the sentence.

"I don't know what to think anymore." Emily sank onto a kitchen stool. "Remember when we were dating, and he surprised me with tickets to that jazz concert I wanted to see? He said he couldn't stand jazz but loved seeing me happy." She laughed bitterly. "Maybe that was the first lie. Maybe he's been playing a part all along."

"Maybe he's just stressed and mixed up the names," Sarah suggested. "People make mistakes when they're tired."

"I need more proof before confronting him." Emily agreed, taking a sip of her coffee.

Sarah nodded slowly. "I might have an idea about that. My ex was paranoid about break-ins after that robbery on Maple Street last year. He bought these small security cameras—they connect to your phone, motion-activated. I still have them."

"You want me to spy on my husband?" Emily's voice caught on the last word.

"I want you to protect yourself," Sarah corrected gently. "If Mark is hiding something significant, you need to know. For your sake and for Claire's."

At the mention of her daughter, Emily's resolve strengthened. Claire was at that precarious age where her perception of relationships would shape her expectations for life. What example was Mark setting? What lessons would their family dynamic teach her?

"What about this storage unit?" Sarah asked, pushing the key forward with her fingertip. "We could try to find out where it is."

"The logo on the key—I think it's for SecureLock Storage on Westfield Road," Emily said. "But I can't just walk in there and try to access his unit. What if they call him?"

"You're right," Sarah agreed. "Better to focus on surveillance first. See if you can catch him in the act, whatever that act might be."

"Bring the cameras," Emily said firmly. "I'll do it."

As Sarah was leaving, she paused at the door. "Emily, if Mark is involved in something illegal... be careful. Really careful. People who launder money aren't usually working alone."

The warning sent a chill down Emily's spine. Could

Mark be part of some larger criminal operation? The thought seemed absurd—her husband, the man who coached Claire's soccer team and meticulously sorted their recycling every Sunday night. And yet, the evidence in her pocket suggested a stranger had been living under her roof all along.

***

The camera was smaller than Emily had expected, hardly larger than a golf ball. Sarah had shown her how to set it up, download the app to her phone, and position it for optimal coverage without being obvious. They'd chosen a spot on the bookshelf in the living room, nestled between a framed family photo from Claire's middle school graduation and a ceramic vase Mark had brought back from a "business trip" to Arizona three years before.

"I got another one for the garage," Sarah said, holding up an identical device. "If he's making those late-night calls from there, we should cover that base, too."

"You think of everything," Emily said gratefully.

"Reporter habits die hard," Sarah replied with a grim smile. "Always look for corroborating evidence."

Emily checked the angle on her phone's screen. Perfect view of the entryway and most of the living room. If Mark was making suspicious calls or bringing anyone into their home, she'd know.

After installing the second camera in the garage, carefully positioned to capture anyone standing near Mark's workbench where she'd heard him talking, Emily and Sarah tested the feed on Emily's phone.

"Crystal clear," Sarah confirmed. "Now we wait."

As Emily adjusted the final settings, a wave of nausea washed over her. This wasn't who they were supposed to be—two people who'd promised honesty, reduced to surveillance and suspicion. She remembered their wedding day, Mark's eyes bright with unshed tears as he promised to cherish her always. Had that been real? Or had he always been this stranger she was now investigating?

A memory surfaced: Mark, two years ago, password-protecting his laptop for the first time. "Client confidentiality," he'd explained. She hadn't questioned it. Then came the separate bank account for "easier expense tracking." The late-night texts he always angled away from her view. The weekend conferences that left no digital footprint she could find.

And now, mysterious storage units, coded ledgers with large sums of money, and notebooks marked with the word "cleaned." The puzzle pieces were starting to form a disturbing picture.

The signs had been there all along, small fractures in the foundation she'd chosen to plaster over rather than examine.

The crunch of tires on gravel jolted her back to the present. Mark's car was pulling into the driveway hours earlier than she expected. Emily frantically gathered the packaging and instructions, shoving them into her tote bag.

"He's home early," she whispered urgently to Sarah.

"You need to leave through the back—I don't want him to know you're here."

Sarah nodded, grabbing her purse. "Call me as soon as you can," she whispered back, slipping out through the kitchen door that led to the backyard.

Her heartbeat thundered in her ears as she heard his key in the lock. She plastered on a smile she didn't feel and prepared to greet the man who now felt like both stranger and spouse—the man whose secrets she was determined to uncover, no matter the cost to the life they'd built together.

"Emily?" Mark called out, his voice echoing through the hallway. "Whose car is that parked down the street? Looks like Sarah's."

Emily's pulse quickened. How did he know Sarah's car by sight? And why was he asking?

"Sarah left a little while ago," she said smoothly. "We had coffee. Why?"

As the door swung open, Emily caught her reflection in the hallway mirror—a woman she barely recognized, with secrets of her own now. The perfect façade of their suburban existence was crumbling, and she alone could see the darkness seeping through the cracks.

Mark's eyes scanned the living room briefly before settling on her. "Just thought I saw her car." He smiled, but there was something calculating in his gaze that Emily had never noticed before. Or perhaps it had always been there, and she simply hadn't been looking.

3

DANGEROUS DISCOVERIES

Emily had been watching Mark's movements through the hidden cameras for three days. Nothing conclusive yet—just a series of late-night phone calls, all taken in the garage, where the audio wasn't clear enough to make out more than fragments. "Shipment," "schedules," and "accounts" were words she'd caught, but without context, they meant little.

This morning, she'd made a decision. Instead of

waiting for evidence to come to her, she would seek it out directly. A surprise visit to Mark's office seemed both innocent enough to explain away if questioned, and potentially revealing if she caught him off-guard.

"I'm bringing lunch to Dad today," she told Claire, who was home from school with a mild cold. "Will you be okay alone for a couple of hours?"

"Mom, I'm sixteen, not six," Claire had responded with typical teenage exasperation. "Besides, Sarah said she'd stop by to drop off that book she promised me."

Emily hesitated. She hadn't told Claire about her suspicions, but having Sarah check in would ease her mind. "Perfect. I shouldn't be long anyway."

Now, as she pulled into the visitor parking at Preston Financial Advisors, Emily felt a flutter of anxiety. Was she crossing a line? But then she thought of the storage unit key hidden in her jewelry box, and the mysterious ledger with its cryptic notations, and she steeled her resolve.

She carried a bag from Mark's favorite deli and wore a casual-but-put-together outfit—nothing that would suggest this was anything other than a thoughtful wife bringing lunch to her hardworking husband. The receptionist greeted her with a smile as she entered the sleek, modern lobby.

"Mrs. Johnson! What a lovely surprise. Mark didn't mention you were coming by today."

"That's because he doesn't know," Emily replied with

an easy laugh. "Thought I'd surprise him with his favorite sandwich. Is he in?"

"He's in a meeting right now, but they should be wrapping up soon. Would you like to wait? I can let him know you're here."

"No, don't tell him," Emily said quickly. "I want it to be a surprise. I'll just wait over there." She gestured to the seating area near the conference rooms.

The receptionist looked hesitant. "Well... all right. They're in Conference Room B, just down that hallway. You should be able to catch him when they finish."

"Thank you," Emily said, moving toward the waiting area. As she walked past Conference Room B, she noticed the door was slightly ajar. Perfect—she could wait nearby and perhaps overhear something useful.

She selected a chair positioned with a clear view of the conference room door but partially obscured by a large plant. As she settled in, voices drifted out from the meeting room, growing louder as someone approached the door.

"Mark's getting careless," a man's voice said clearly. "The last shipment had discrepancies that are hard to explain away."

Emily froze, a sandwich bag clutched in her suddenly clammy hands.

"He's under pressure," a second voice responded. "The Johnson account is drawing attention. Timing couldn't be worse."

Johnson account? Emily's pulse quickened. Johnson was their surname—was this some kind of code?

"Tom's handling the fallout, but we need Mark to clean up his trail. The audit—"

The voices fell silent as the door swung fully open. Three men in business casual attire emerged, one flipping through documents while another scrolled through his phone. The third was looking back into the room, speaking to someone still inside.

Emily lowered her gaze to her phone, angling her face away while trying to listen. Through her peripheral vision, she recognized the third man as he turned—the same face from the photo in Mark's desk. Tom Mitchell.

"—not sustainable," Tom was saying to whoever remained in the room. "We've covered too many transactions already. If his wife starts asking questions—"

"She won't," another voice interrupted—Mark's voice. "Emily's completely in the dark. Besides, we've got enough leverage to ensure everyone stays quiet."

Emily's mind raced, trying to connect these disparate threads into a coherent picture. This wasn't just about infidelity or petty secrets; the conversation hinted at something far more sinister. Financial impropriety, at a minimum. Possibly worse.

What the hell was going on here?

"The transfer needs to happen by Tuesday," Tom continued, his voice dropping further as the group moved toward the elevator bank. "After that, we clean house, and nobody asks questions. The kind of cleaning that leaves no traces, if you understand me."

The implication in his tone made Emily's blood run cold. Before she could process what she'd heard, the receptionist's voice cut through her thoughts.

"Mrs. Johnson? Your husband is available now, if you'd like to see him."

Emily hadn't noticed her approach from the front desk. Her heart hammered against her ribs. Mark was still in the conference room, alone now. She hadn't planned on actually overhearing anything—this visit was supposed to be reconnaissance only. To see how he felt about her randomly showing up at work. But now she had to play the role of loving wife bringing lunch, all while processing the bombshell she'd just overheard.

"Thank you," she managed, rising on unsteady legs. She smoothed her skirt and approached the conference room, forcing a smile as she stepped into the doorway.

Mark was gathering papers, his back to her. When he turned at the sound of her entry, Emily caught a fleeting expression—something hard and cold—before his face transformed into a mask of pleasant surprise.

"Emily! What are you doing here?" His tone was warm, but she noticed how quickly he closed the folder in front of him and slipped it into his briefcase.

"Thought I'd surprise you with lunch," she said,

holding up the bag with a cheerfulness she didn't feel. "Your favorite from Romano's."

"That's... really thoughtful." Mark crossed the room and kissed her cheek. "But I actually have another meeting across town in twenty minutes. Rain check?"

"Of course," Emily said, fighting to keep her voice steady. "I should have called first."

"No, it's a lovely gesture." Mark took the bag anyway. "I'll eat it in the car. Walk me out?"

Emily nodded, hyperaware of how he placed a guiding hand on her lower back, a gesture that once felt protective but now seemed controlling. As they walked through the office, Mark greeted colleagues with easy charm. No one would suspect that minutes earlier, he had been discussing "cleaning" operations and keeping his wife in the dark.

At the elevator, Mark pressed the down button and turned to her. "Everything okay at home? How's Claire's cold?"

"Getting better," Emily replied automatically. "Sarah's stopping by to check on her."

Something flickered in Mark's eyes at the mention of Sarah. "Sarah's at our house a lot lately."

"She's my best friend," Emily said, studying his reaction. "Is that a problem?"

"No, of course not." The elevator doors opened, and Mark stepped inside. "I'll try not to be too late tonight. Love you."

As the doors closed on his smiling face, Emily felt a chill run through her body. The man she'd just spoken to was a stranger wearing her husband's familiar face.

She made her way back to her car on autopilot, her mind whirling with fragments of the conversation she'd overheard. The "Johnson account." Discrepancies in shipments. Cleaning that leaves no traces. And most disturbing of all—Mark's confident assertion that she was "completely in the dark."

Not anymore, she thought grimly as she started her car. Not anymore.

***

Miller Park stretched before Emily, its sprawling green expanse dotted with weekend visitors—families on picnic blankets, joggers circling the lake, children chasing after frisbees. The normality of the scene felt jarring against the turmoil in her mind.

She spotted Sarah near the east entrance, pacing slightly beside the ornate iron gate. Even from a distance, Emily could see the concern etched on her friend's face.

"Let's walk," Sarah suggested as soon as Emily approached, already steering them toward the lakeside path. "Easier to talk without being overheard."

They fell into step along the gravel trail, the rhythmic crunch beneath their feet providing a steady backbeat to their conversation.

"What happened?" Sarah asked once they'd put some

distance between themselves and the nearest group of parkgoers.

Emily recounted her office visit in detail, her voice low and urgent as she described the overheard conversation between Tom and the other men, followed by her uncomfortable encounter with Mark.

"They specifically mentioned a 'Johnson account,'" Emily concluded. "Johnson—our last name. It can't be a coincidence."

"And you're certain they said Mark needed to 'clean up his trail'?" Sarah asked, guiding them toward a less-trafficked path beneath a canopy of oak trees.

Emily nodded, eyes scanning their surroundings. "Positive. I recognized Tom from photos. And then there was that part about 'cleaning house' in a way that 'leaves no traces.'"

Sarah slowed her pace, considering the implications. "This sounds serious, Em. Far beyond an affair or minor deception. This sounds like something illegal—possibly criminal."

The realization had been forming in Emily's mind since the office visit, but hearing Sarah say it aloud made it terrifyingly real. Around them, birds chirped and children laughed, the peaceful scene a stark contrast to the darkness of their conversation.

"What do I do? Go to the police?" Emily asked. "But with what evidence—an overheard conversation? I don't even know what they're up to."

"Not yet," Sarah cautioned, guiding Emily to a secluded bench overlooking the water. They sat, watching ripples spread across the lake's surface while a duck landed gracefully. "You need more concrete evidence first. But you also need to be careful. If Mark or these men realize you're onto them..."

She didn't finish the sentence. She didn't need to.

"The storage unit," Emily said suddenly. "Whatever Mark's hiding, there might be evidence there. I still have the key."

"That's risky," Sarah warned. "If they're monitoring access to that unit..."

"It might be our best lead. The cameras haven't given us anything conclusive yet."

"Maybe," Sarah conceded reluctantly.

"And what about the neighbors?" Emily asked, watching a pair of elderly joggers pass by on the opposite shore. "Frank Peterson has been watching our house. And I noticed the Millers driving by slowly yesterday evening."

"Probably just normal neighborhood nosiness," Sarah said dismissively. "Small suburban dramas are the lifeblood of people like Frank. I wouldn't worry about them when we have bigger concerns."

"You're probably right," Emily agreed, though everything still unsettled her.

"I can't just sit back and do nothing," Emily said,

anger flaring suddenly through her fear. "This is my life, my family. If Mark is involved in something illegal, Claire and I could be at risk, too."

"Then be strategic," Sarah advised, her voice barely audible above the rustling leaves. "Continue gathering evidence, but protect yourself and Claire first. Maybe set up some kind of... insurance. Information stored somewhere safe, accessible if something happens."

Emily stared at her friend, momentarily taken aback by the calculating suggestion. It seemed uncharacteristically paranoid for Sarah, who typically approached problems with optimism. But, then again, nothing about this situation was typical.

"I feel so powerless," Emily admitted, her voice catching as she watched a young family pass by, the parents holding hands while their toddler threw bread crumbs into the water. "One minute I'm living my normal life, and the next I'm spying on my husband, suspecting criminal activity, and fearing for my safety. How did we get here, Sarah?"

"By trusting the wrong people," Sarah replied softly, her gaze fixed on the distant tree line. "But you're not powerless, Em. You're one of the strongest women I know. And right now, that strength is your greatest asset."

"So, what if I find something in the storage unit?"

Sarah's expression grew serious. "Then we take it to someone we can trust. Maybe that detective your brother knows—what's his name?"

"Ramirez," Emily supplied. "Detective John Ramirez."

"Right. But only when we have enough evidence. For now, we gather information and stay safe."

Emily nodded slowly. They resumed their walk around the lake, a plan beginning to form in her mind— careful steps to uncover the truth while protecting herself and Claire from whatever storm was brewing around them.

4

A HIDDEN LIFE

The storage unit key weighed heavily in Emily's pocket as she drove to SecureLock Storage on Westfield Road. She needed to see for herself what Mark was hiding. The facility was larger than she'd expected—rows of identical orange doors stretching across a sprawling concrete complex. She double-checked the key tag: Unit #47.

The area was deserted, with only the distant sound of traffic from the highway breaking the silence. Good—no witnesses.

She approached the orange roll-up door cautiously,

checking over her shoulder before inserting the key into the padlock. It turned smoothly, and the lock clicked open.

For a brief moment, Emily hesitated. Opening this door could change everything. Whatever lay beyond would transform her suspicions into concrete reality, her fears into facts. There would be no going back to blissful ignorance.

Was she ready to see what her husband had been hiding from her? She'd seen enough TV to wonder if she was about to find a dead body strung up or piles of dirty money stacked neatly in suitcases.

I need to know, she decided.

She took a deep breath and lifted the door.

The musty smell hit her first—the scent of papers and dust and secrets. While her eyes adjusted to the dim light filtering through a small overhead window, Emily stepped inside, letting the door close partially behind her.

The unit was smaller than she'd expected, perhaps ten by fifteen feet. Unlike the chaotic stash of illegal goods she'd half-anticipated, the space was meticulously organized. A metal desk stood against one wall, flanked by filing cabinets. Opposite sat a small table with what looked like computer equipment, currently powered down. A swivel chair was pushed neatly under the desk.

This wasn't just storage—this was an office. A secret workspace Mark had established completely outside their home.

Emily moved to the desk first, running her fingers

along its cool metal surface. A yellow legal pad sat on top, covered with handwritten notes in Mark's distinctive scrawl. Most appeared to be calculations and abbreviations that meant nothing to her. But a section circled in red caught her eye:

Johnson-Reynolds pipeline confirmed. 400K transferred via usual channels. TR wants higher cut for "cleaning" services. Risky to negotiate now with audit pending.

Emily's breath caught. Johnson-Reynolds. Their last name paired with a familiar one—Reynolds was Claire's middle name, chosen to honor Emily's grandmother and Emily's maiden name. Mark was using their family names as some kind of code for his operations.

With trembling hands, she opened the top desk drawer. Inside lay several burner phones still in their packaging, a stack of prepaid credit cards, and a ledger similar to the one she'd photographed in Mark's home office, but covering different dates.

The second drawer contained folders labeled with initials and numbers. She pulled one at random—JM-117— and opened it to find what appeared to be false invoices for consulting services, along with bank statements showing transfers of large sums.

The bottom drawer was locked. Emily tried the storage unit key, but it didn't fit. She'd need to look elsewhere.

Moving to the filing cabinets, she found more folders

that were organized by date rather than initials. She selected one from three months ago and began scanning its contents. What she found made her blood run cold.

The documents detailed an elaborate financial scheme. Mark's firm was accepting "investments" from clients that were actually illegal funds. The money would be moved through a series of shell companies, "cleaned" through legitimate-seeming transactions, and returned to the clients minus a substantial commission. Emily's stomach dropped as she recognized the hallmarks of money laundering from those true crime shows she'd binged last year.

The operation was clearly sophisticated and involved multiple accomplices, including someone identified only as "TM," who appeared to handle the "cleaning" process.

Tom Mitchell. The man from Mark's office.

Emily's head swam while the pieces fell into place. This wasn't about infidelity. Mark wasn't having an affair; he was running a criminal enterprise, using his position at Preston Financial to launder money for what appeared to be some very dangerous people.

A folder labeled "Insurance" caught her attention. Inside were photographs—surveillance photos of various people, including some of Mark's colleagues. Emily recognized Jeff from the Christmas party, photographed meeting with someone in a parked car. Another showed a woman Emily didn't know, clearly distressed, handing over an envelope. These weren't romantic liaisons; they were blackmail material.

One final photo made her gasp aloud—it showed her and Claire shopping at the mall last month. Someone had been watching them. Mark had been watching them. Or perhaps using them as his own insurance policy. The thought made her physically ill.

Her hands shaking, she replaced the folder and continued her search, finding offshore account numbers, identity documents with Mark's photo but different names, and a small notebook with contact information—names and numbers without context, potential accomplices, or victims.

On the small table with the computer equipment, she found something even more disturbing—a voice recorder with a Post-it note reading "J.R. meeting—leverage?" She pressed play, and a conversation filled the small space:

"I don't care what you have to do. Get it done." Mark's voice, hard and cold in a way she'd never heard before.

"This goes beyond our agreement." Another male voice, stressed and angry. "You said clean transactions only, nothing that could—"

"You're already implicated. We all are. And I have the records to prove it."

"Is that a threat?"

"It's a reality check. Do your job, and we all profit. Hesitate, and I'll make sure you're the first one they look at when this comes apart."

The recording ended, leaving Emily in stunned

silence. This was blackmail—Mark threatening a colleague to keep him in line. How many others were involved against their will?

The sound of a car door slamming outside jolted Emily back to reality. She quickly replaced everything as she'd found it, her heart racing. She needed to leave—now.

Slipping out of the unit, she locked it and hurried toward her car, keys clutched tightly in her sweating palm. As she rounded the corner of the building, she nearly collided with a man walking in the opposite direction.

"I'm sorry," she mumbled, keeping her head down while she tried to move past.

"Mrs. Johnson?"

Emily froze. Slowly, she raised her eyes to meet the curious gaze of Frank Peterson, her neighbor.

"Mr. Peterson. What a... coincidence," she managed, forcing a smile.

"Indeed." His eyes flicked toward the storage units, then back to her face. "Picking something up for Mark?"

"Yes. Just some old tax records he needed." The lie came easily now, practiced from days of pretending everything was normal at home.

Frank smiled, but it didn't reach his eyes. "Of course. Well, don't let me keep you."

Emily nodded and continued to her car, feeling his gaze burning into her back. Her mind raced with questions. What was Frank doing here? Was it truly a coincidence, or was he watching her? Was he involved somehow?

Once inside her car, doors locked, Emily pulled out her phone with trembling fingers and called Sarah.

"I found it," she whispered as soon as Sarah answered. "It's worse than we thought, much worse. And Sarah—Frank Peterson was here. He saw me."

"Get out of there now," Sarah's voice was urgent. "Come straight to my place. Don't go home."

"I need to pick up Claire from school—"

"Text Claire to go to a friend's house. Say you had an emergency. Just don't go home until we figure this out."

Emily started the car, her mind still reeling from everything she'd discovered. "Sarah, Mark is laundering money. And he's blackmailing people. There were photos—of Claire and me. He's been watching us."

"Jesus," Sarah breathed. "This is way beyond what we thought. Did you take anything? Any evidence?"

"I took photos with my phone. I left everything else exactly as I found it."

"Good. Now get out of there, and we'll figure out next steps."

Emily pulled out of the parking lot, checking her rearview mirror compulsively. No sign of Frank Peterson following her, but that didn't mean he wasn't reporting her presence to someone else—or to Mark.

Her entire world had collapsed in the space of thirty minutes. Her husband was a criminal. Their family was under surveillance. And now, a neighbor had caught her investigating. The danger felt suddenly immediate and overwhelming.

***

Emily sat in Sarah's kitchen, a cup of untouched tea growing cold before her. She'd shown Sarah the photos she'd taken of the storage unit contents, and they'd spent the past hour piecing together the scope of Mark's operation.

"It's sophisticated," Sarah said, scrolling through the images on Emily's phone. "This isn't amateur hour. Mark knows what he's doing."

"But why?" Emily's voice broke. "We have a good life. He makes good money legitimately. Why risk everything like this?"

"Power? Greed? Who knows?" Sarah set down the phone. "The question is, what are you going to do now?"

Emily stared into her tea, watching the faint ripples on its surface. The person she'd believed Mark to be—loving husband, devoted father, hardworking financial advisor—had vanished, replaced by a stranger who threatened colleagues and used his own family as collateral. How could she have been so blind?

"I should go to the police," she said finally.

"With what? Photos that could have been taken anywhere? They'll need more than that, especially if Mark has connections." Sarah leaned forward. "And if he's as dangerous as this suggests, going to the wrong person could be risky."

"Then what? I can't just go home and pretend everything is normal. Not after this."

"You have to—at least for now." Sarah's expression was grave. "For Claire's sake, if nothing else. If Mark suspects you know something, there's no telling what he might do."

Emily's chest tightened at the thought of Claire. "I can't just do nothing. He's using our names—Johnson, Reynolds—as code for his money-laundering operation. Our family is part of this, whether we know it or not."

"Then we get more evidence," Sarah insisted. "Enough that the police can't ignore it. And we find someone trustworthy to take it to."

Emily nodded slowly, her mind drifting back to the man she'd seen at the storage facility. "What about Frank Peterson? Do you think he's involved?"

"It's possible. Or he could just be Mark's eyes in the neighborhood." Sarah frowned. "Either way, you need to be careful around him."

"The whole neighborhood could be watching," Emily realized with a chill. "The Millers, Lisa Turner... anyone could be reporting back to Mark."

"All the more reason to act normal while we figure this out," Sarah urged. "You need to go home, be with Claire, and pretend nothing has changed. Can you do that?"

Could she? Could she sit across from Mark at dinner, knowing what he really was? Sleep beside him, knowing he'd used their family names for criminal activities? Smile at neighbors who might be spying on her?

"I don't know," she admitted, tears finally spilling down her cheeks. "Everything feels... contaminated. Our whole life together feels like a lie."

Sarah moved to sit beside her, wrapping an arm around her shoulders. "I know. And I'm so sorry, Em. But you're stronger than you realize. You've uncovered all this on your own. That took courage and smarts—the same qualities that will get you and Claire through this."

Emily wiped her tears, drawing a shaky breath. "I should go," she said, gathering her things. "Claire will be wondering where I am."

"Call me later," Sarah insisted. "And Emily? Do not confront Mark. Not yet. Not until we have a plan."

Emily nodded, though part of her wanted nothing more than to face her husband with what she knew, to demand explanations for every betrayal. But Sarah was right—she needed to be strategic. For now, she would continue the charade, playing the role of oblivious wife while gathering evidence that would eventually expose Mark's double life.

While she drove home, Emily couldn't shake the feeling that she was being watched. Every car that lingered too long behind her seemed suspicious; every pedestrian glancing her way felt like a potential threat. The quiet suburban streets that had once felt safe now seemed sinister, hiding secrets behind manicured lawns and pristine facades.

Her own home—the one she'd lovingly decorated, where she'd raised her daughter and built a life—now felt like enemy territory. A place where every corner might conceal surveillance, where the man she'd married operated a criminal enterprise under her nose.

But beneath her fear, a new emotion was taking root: determination. Mark had lied to her, used her, and potentially put her and Claire in danger. She would not remain a pawn in his game. Somehow, she would find a way to protect herself and her daughter, and to bring Mark's operation crashing down around him.

5

ALLIES AND ADVERSARIES

The kitchen was filled with the rich **aroma** of Mark's favorite lasagna, a recipe Emily had perfected over the years. She moved methodically through the familiar routine—setting the table, uncorking wine, arranging garlic bread in a basket—while her mind raced with everything she'd discovered in the storage unit. Two days had passed, and maintaining the facade of normalcy had become its own kind of torture.

"Something smells amazing," Mark called as the front door closed behind him. His footsteps approached the kitchen, each one making Emily's pulse quicken slightly.

"Lasagna," she replied, forcing lightness into her voice. "Thought we could use a nice dinner, just the two of us. Claire's at Jenna's for a study group."

Mark appeared in the doorway, loosening his tie with one hand while the other held his briefcase—the same briefcase she'd seen him hastily stuff documents into at his office. His smile seemed genuine as he crossed the kitchen to kiss her cheek.

"What's the occasion?" he asked, pouring himself a glass of wine.

Emily shrugged, carefully cutting the lasagna into perfect squares. "No occasion. Just felt like cooking."

Mark studied her for a moment, something calculating behind his eyes that she'd never noticed before—or perhaps had never looked for. "You seem tense lately. Everything okay?"

"Just busy with work," she lied. "Always gets hectic this time of year."

They settled at the table, the familiar domestic scene now feeling like an elaborate performance. Emily sipped her wine, watching Mark over the rim of her glass. This man she'd shared a bed with for fifteen years, the father of her child, was a stranger—a criminal who used their family names as code for illegal activities.

"How's your day?" she asked, the mundane question feeling absurd under the circumstances.

"Productive." Mark stabbed the pasta with his fork. "Though Tom's been riding me about some discrepancies in the quarterly reports. Nothing major, just tedious reconciliation work."

Emily's stomach clenched at the mention of Tom, remembering his words at the office: *"Mark's getting careless."* She wondered what "discrepancies" really meant in their criminal enterprise.

"Sounds stressful," she offered neutrally.

"It's fine." Mark waved dismissively. "Speaking of stress, you haven't seemed yourself lately. Is it the migraines?"

"It's just work stuff," she said, the lie coming easier now with practice.

"Right." Mark nodded slowly. "Well, if there's anything bothering you, you know you can tell me. We're partners in everything, Em."

The irony of his words wasn't lost on her. Partners—except for the secret criminal enterprise he ran, the threats he made, the people he blackmailed.

"Actually," Emily began carefully, "I've been thinking about setting up a separate account for Claire's college fund. Move it out of our joint savings into something with better interest rates."

Mark's fork paused halfway to his mouth. "Any

particular reason?"

"Just being practical. She'll be applying to schools before we know it."

"I can handle that," Mark said smoothly. "I have access to some excellent investment vehicles through work. Much better returns than a standard account."

Emily forced a smile. "I'd like to do it myself, actually. Give me a project to focus on besides work."

"Emily." Mark set down his fork, his voice gentle but firm. "Financial planning is literally my job. Let me handle it."

"I know, but—"

"I insist." His smile remained, but something in his eyes hardened. "In fact, I think we should consolidate more of our accounts. It's not efficient having money scattered across different banks."

Emily recognized the tactic for what it was—an attempt to maintain control, to limit her financial independence. Had he always been this controlling, or was she only now seeing it through the lens of her discoveries?

"Maybe you're right," she conceded, knowing direct confrontation would only make him suspicious. "We can discuss it this weekend."

Mark's posture relaxed slightly. "Good. I only want what's best for our family—you know that."

"Of course." Emily took another sip of wine to hide her expression. "By the way, I ran into Frank Peterson yesterday. He mentioned seeing you at the gym."

It was a calculated risk—Mark rarely went to the gym, and Emily knew it. She watched carefully for his reaction.

Mark didn't miss a beat. "Yeah, trying to get back into a routine. Doctor said my cholesterol's creeping up."

Another lie. His last physical had shown perfect health—Emily had gone with him. The ease with which falsehoods rolled off his tongue was chilling.

"Sarah mentioned meeting Tom's wife at a charity thing last month," Emily continued, testing another angle. "Said she seemed nice."

This time, Mark's eyes narrowed almost imperceptibly. "Tom's not married."

"Oh? I must have misunderstood." Emily feigned confusion. "She said something about meeting Tom's wife or girlfriend... maybe it was someone else."

"Sarah seems very interested in my colleagues lately," Mark remarked, his tone light, but his eyes were watchful. "First asking about the Henderson project when we ran into her at Rosetti's, now this."

Emily's blood ran cold. She and Sarah had discussed the Henderson account in private—how did Mark know Sarah had asked about it?

"You know Sarah," Emily said with forced nonchalance. "Always networking."

"Hmm." Mark took another bite of lasagna. "This is delicious, by the way. You've outdone yourself."

"Thanks." Emily smiled, her mind racing. Either Sarah had spoken to Mark directly, or... their conversations were being monitored somehow.

"Oh, I almost forgot," Mark said, reaching for his phone. "I need to set up that security system upgrade I mentioned. The tech can come tomorrow morning."

Emily tensed. The cameras she and Sarah had installed were well-hidden, but a professional security review might find them. Was this Mark's way of sweeping for surveillance? "What upgrade?" she asked tensely. "The system's only two years old."

"The company's offering free enhancements to existing customers. More cameras, better monitoring. Given the break-ins on Maple Street last month, I figured better safe than sorry."

More cameras. Better monitoring. Emily's skin crawled at the implications.

"I can handle it if you're busy," she offered, desperate to prevent additional surveillance in their home.

"No need. Already scheduled." Mark's smile didn't reach his eyes. "After all, keeping our family safe is my top priority."

The words hung between them, and for the first time, Emily heard the threat beneath the concern. Mark wasn't just talking about external dangers—he was sending her a message.

Later, as they cleared the table together in a parody of

domestic harmony, Mark's phone buzzed with a text. He checked it quickly, frowning.

"Everything okay?" Emily asked, loading plates into the dishwasher.

"Just work. I need to go in early tomorrow." He slipped the phone back into his pocket. "Don't wait up for me tonight. I have to review some documents that just came in."

"On a Friday night?" Emily kept her tone light, curious rather than accusatory.

Mark's hand settled on her shoulder, squeezing gently. "The price of success, I'm afraid. But it's all for us—for you and Claire." His fingers tightened almost imperceptibly. "I'd do anything to protect what we have. You know that, right?"

Emily looked up at the face of the man she'd once trusted implicitly, seeing now the calculated intensity behind his affectionate expression. "I know," she said softly.

His hand lingered a moment longer than necessary, the pressure just shy of uncomfortable, before he released her and headed upstairs to his office.

Alone in the kitchen, Emily leaned against the counter, her heart racing. The exchange had confirmed her worst fears—Mark suspected something. The mention of the security system "upgrade," the veiled warnings about protecting their family... he was watching her. Possibly listening, too.

And Sarah—was she truly an ally? Mark's comment about her asking questions raised disturbing possibilities. Could Sarah be reporting back to Mark? Or was he fishing for information, trying to determine how much Emily had shared with her friend?

One thing was clear: Emily needed help from someone outside their immediate circle. Someone with authority and resources. Someone who couldn't be easily manipulated or threatened by Mark.

She pulled out her phone, scrolling through contacts until she found the number her brother had given her months ago after a minor fender-bender—Detective John Ramirez. At the time, she'd thought it excessive to have a police contact for a simple traffic incident. Now, it felt like a lifeline.

The next morning, while Mark was at his "early meeting," she would take the first step toward breaking free from the web of lies surrounding her marriage. Whatever the consequences, she couldn't continue living in fear, wondering which parts of her life were real and which were manipulated by the stranger she'd married.

***

The police station bustled with activity as Emily pushed through the glass doors the next morning. Officers in uniform moved purposefully between desks, phones rang continuously, and the atmosphere hummed with a sense of urgency that matched her internal state.

At the front desk, a harried-looking officer barely glanced up from his computer. "How can I help you?"

"I'm here to see Detective Ramirez. John Ramirez." Emily's voice came out steadier than she felt. "My name is Emily Johnson."

"Do you have an appointment?"

"No, but it's important. My brother, Mike Collins, gave me his contact information."

The officer typed something, then nodded. "Have a seat. I'll let him know you're here."

Emily perched on a hard plastic chair in the waiting area, clutching her purse, which contained printouts of the photos she'd taken at the storage unit. She'd been careful, using the printer at a copy shop rather than at home or work, paying cash, and storing the originals in a secure cloud account only she could access.

Twenty minutes passed, each second amplifying her anxiety. What if Ramirez couldn't help? What if Mark had connections in the police department? What if—

"Mrs. Johnson?"

Emily looked up to see a man in his late thirties with a neatly trimmed beard and watchful brown eyes. He didn't match the stereotypical detective from TV shows—no rumpled suit or world-weary expression—but something in his careful assessment of her suggested experience beyond his years.

"Detective Ramirez?" Emily stood, extending her hand.

He shook it firmly. "Mike's sister, right? He mentioned you might call someday. Though I admit, I expected it would be about a speeding ticket, not..." He gestured vaguely. "Whatever brings you here looking this concerned?"

"Is there somewhere we can talk privately?" Emily asked, glancing around the busy station.

Ramirez studied her for a moment, then nodded. "Follow me."

He led her through a maze of desks to a small interview room with minimal furnishings—a table, three chairs, and blank walls. No windows, just a door that Ramirez closed behind them, offering at least the illusion of privacy.

"So," he said, settling into a chair across from her. "What's this about?"

Emily hesitated. Once she spoke, there would be no going back. Her carefully constructed life would begin its inevitable unraveling.

"I believe my husband is involved in criminal activity," she said finally, the words hanging in the sterile air between them. "Money laundering, possibly blackmail. And I have evidence."

If Ramirez was surprised, he didn't show it. His expression remained neutral, professional. "That's a serious accusation, Mrs. Johnson. Especially against a spouse."

"I know how it sounds." Emily leaned forward. "But I wouldn't be here if I weren't certain."

"And your husband is...?"

"Mark Johnson. He's a financial advisor at Preston Financial."

Something flickered in Ramirez's eyes—recognition, perhaps, or concern. "I see. And what led you to believe he's involved in criminal activity?"

Emily took a deep breath and began recounting the events of the past weeks—the suspicious text message, the conflicting stories about work, the discovery of the storage unit key, and finally, what she'd found inside Unit #47. She detailed everything, including the names of everyone involved—Sarah, Tom, even Claire.

As she spoke, Ramirez took notes, his expression giving away nothing. When she finished, he sat back, tapping his pen against his notepad.

"Do you have any of this evidence with you?"

Emily reached into her purse and pulled out the envelope of printouts. "These are copies of photos I took inside the storage unit. I also have digital backups stored securely."

Ramirez spread the photos across the table, examining each one carefully. His professionalism couldn't quite mask his growing interest as he studied the ledgers, the coded references to "Johnson-Reynolds," and the surveillance photos.

"Your husband took surveillance photos of you and your daughter?" he asked, his voice carefully neutral.

"Yes. Or had someone take them. Either way, they were in his possession, in a folder labeled 'Insurance.'"

Ramirez gathered the photos back into the envelope. "Mrs. Johnson, I want to be straightforward with you. These photos suggest potentially serious financial crimes, but they're not conclusive evidence on their own. We'd need more—account records, witness statements, concrete proof of illegal transactions."

Emily's heart sank. "So you can't help me?"

"I didn't say that." Ramirez leaned forward. "What I'm saying is that building a case like this takes time and careful work. Especially if your husband is as sophisticated as this suggests."

"I don't have time," Emily said, frustration edging her voice. "He knows something's wrong. He's installing new security cameras in our house, making veiled threats about 'protecting our family.' I'm afraid for myself and my daughter."

Ramirez's expression softened slightly. "Has he ever been physically violent?"

"No, never. But I've never threatened his... operation before. I don't know what he's capable of."

The detective was quiet for a moment, seemingly weighing options. "Do you have somewhere safe you and your daughter could stay, if necessary?"

"My brother's, maybe. Or Sarah's, if she's not..." Emily trailed off, the doubts about her friend still troubling her.

"If she's not what?"

Emily hesitated, then explained her concerns about Sarah based on Mark's comments at dinner. "It could be nothing. He might be trying to isolate me, make me doubt the people I trust."

"That's a common tactic," Ramirez agreed. "But it's also prudent to be cautious. If your husband is involved in organized financial crime, his network could be extensive."

He pulled a business card from his pocket and wrote a number on the back. "This is my direct line. If you ever feel you're in immediate danger, call 911 first, then me."

Emily took the card, turning it over in her fingers. "So, what happens now?"

"Now, I do some preliminary investigation. Quietly." Ramirez's expression was serious. "I need to verify some of what you've told me, check if Preston Financial has come up in any other investigations, see what we know about Tom Mitchell."

"And then?"

"Then we meet again, compare notes, and determine next steps." He hesitated. "Mrs. Johnson—Emily—I need to ask. Are you prepared for what might happen if these allegations prove true? Your husband could face serious charges. Your finances, your home—everything could be impacted."

Emily thought of Claire, of the life they'd built, of the fifteen years she'd devoted to a marriage that now seemed built on quicksand. "I don't have a choice. Whatever happens, living with the truth has to be better than living with lies."

Ramirez nodded, seemingly satisfied with her answer. "One more thing. Do you have the key to that storage unit?"

"Yes," Emily confirmed, reaching into her purse to show him.

"Keep it secure but accessible. Don't return to the unit alone, but we may need to document its contents officially at some point."

They stood, and Ramirez escorted her back through the station. He paused at the door. "Act normal at home. Don't confront your husband or give any indication that you've spoken to police. If he's as connected as you suspect, any change in your behavior could alert him."

"I understand." Emily squared her shoulders. "Detective Ramirez? Thank you for believing me."

"I haven't reached any conclusions yet," he corrected gently. "But I promise to investigate thoroughly. That's my job."

As Emily walked to her car, she felt both lighter and heavier—relieved to have shared her burden with someone who might actually be able to help, yet weighed down by the reality of what lay ahead. The simple act of walking into the police station had set in motion events that would forever change her life, Claire's life, and the lives of everyone connected to Mark's activities.

Back in her car, Emily checked her phone and found three missed calls from Sarah and a text:

Need to talk ASAP. Important.

A kernel of doubt took root as she remembered Mark's insinuations about Sarah asking questions about his work. Was this urgent need to talk related to something Sarah had learned—or something Mark had instructed her to find out?

Before she could decide whether to respond, her phone rang with a number she didn't recognize. Hesitantly, she answered.

"Mrs. Johnson? This is Detective Ramirez. I know we just spoke, but something's come up. I need you to come back to the station right away."

"What is it?" Emily asked, anxiety flooding back.

"I'd rather not discuss it over the phone. How quickly can you get back here?"

"Fifteen minutes," she said, already starting the car.

"Good. Come to the side entrance this time. I'll meet you there."

The call ended, leaving Emily with a sense of foreboding. What could have developed so quickly after their meeting? Had Ramirez found something that confirmed her suspicions? Or had something happened to put her in greater danger?

As she pulled out of the parking lot, she noticed a familiar car two spaces down—Frank Peterson's blue sedan. Coincidence? Or had he followed her to the police station? Either way, she needed to get back to Ramirez and find out what new development had made him call her back so urgently.

***

The side entrance of the police station was quieter than the main lobby, with only a uniformed officer monitoring access. Ramirez was waiting just inside, his expression grave.

"Thank you for coming back so quickly," he said, leading her down a different corridor than before.

"What's happened?" Emily asked, struggling to keep pace with his long strides.

"After you left, I ran some preliminary searches. Preston Financial has come up in a few reports—nothing concrete, but enough to raise flags." He stopped outside a door marked "Evidence Review." "But that's not why I called you back. We received some surveillance footage I think you should see."

Inside the room, a computer was set up with a paused video on screen. Ramirez closed the door and gestured for Emily to sit.

"This was captured two days ago at The Grand Hotel downtown. Part of an ongoing surveillance operation unrelated to your case, but when you mentioned Tom Mitchell during our conversation, I ran his name through our system, and this footage was flagged."

He pressed play, and Emily watched as Tom Mitchell entered the hotel's bar, followed moments later by a woman with chestnut hair. The camera angle made it difficult to see her face clearly until she turned to order a drink.

Emily's breath caught.

Sarah.

Her best friend, her confidante, the person she'd trusted with her darkest suspicions about Mark, was meeting with Tom Mitchell—not bumping into him by accident, but deliberately sitting beside him at the bar, engaging in what appeared to be an intense conversation.

"It might be innocent," Ramirez said, watching Emily's face carefully. "But given your concerns..."

"Play more," Emily said, her voice barely above a whisper.

The footage continued, showing Sarah and Tom talking for nearly twenty minutes. At one point, Sarah passed something to Tom—a small envelope that he quickly tucked into his jacket. Then they separated, leaving the bar through different exits approximately three minutes apart.

"There's more," Ramirez said quietly, pulling up another video file. "This was taken yesterday, outside your house."

The grainy footage showed Sarah's car parked across the street. But instead of approaching Emily's front door, Sarah moved to Frank Peterson's house, entering without knocking. Minutes later, Mark's car appeared, and he, too, entered the Peterson residence.

Emily felt physically ill, the betrayal hitting her like a physical blow. "She's working with them. With Mark."

"Possibly," Ramirez agreed.

The reality crashed over Emily in waves. Sarah had been her closest friend for years, the person she'd turned to when her suspicions about Mark first arose. Sarah had suggested the cameras, encouraged her to investigate the storage unit, and had been privy to every discovery, every fear, every plan.

"Oh, god," Emily whispered, the implications sinking in. "She knows everything. She's been monitoring me for him this whole time."

Ramirez placed a hand on her shoulder. "Mrs. Johnson, given this development, I think we need to accelerate our timeline. If your husband has people watching you, including someone as close as Sarah, your situation may be more precarious than we initially thought."

Emily nodded numbly, her mind racing through every conversation with Sarah, every piece of advice her "friend" had given her. Had any of it been genuine? Or had Sarah been manipulating her from the start, guiding her investigation in directions Mark wanted, gathering information about what Emily knew and suspected?

"What do I do now?" she asked, hearing the tremor in her voice.

"First, we need to ensure your safety and your daughter's. Then, we need to gather more concrete evidence of the criminal operation." Ramirez leaned forward. "But, most importantly, you need to continue acting normally. If Sarah or Mark suspect that you know about their connection, it could force their hand."

"I'm supposed to have coffee with Sarah tomorrow," Emily said, the ordinary plan now feeling like walking into a trap.

"Keep that appointment," Ramirez advised. "Act natural. But be careful what you share with her."

"And Mark?"

"The same. Normal routines, normal conversations. Meanwhile, I'll expedite our investigation." He handed her another card. "This is the contact information for a victims' advocate who works with the department. She can help with safety planning, temporary accommodations, if needed, and other resources."

Emily took the card automatically, still reeling from the revelation about Sarah. "I trusted her completely," she said, more to herself than to Ramirez. "She was like family."

"I'm sorry," Ramirez said, and the simple sincerity in

his voice nearly broke Emily's carefully maintained composure. "Betrayal by those closest to us is always the hardest to bear."

As Emily prepared to leave, a new wave of anxiety washed over her. "If Sarah's working with Mark, and she knows I've been investigating him, why haven't they stopped me? Why let me find the storage unit, discover the evidence?"

Ramirez considered this, his expression troubled. "There could be several explanations. Perhaps they're building a case against you, making it seem like you're the one involved in illegal activities. Or they're using you to identify potential threats to their operation. Or..."

"Or what?"

"Or they want you to find exactly what they've allowed you to find, for reasons we don't yet understand." He met her gaze directly. "Which means we need to be extremely careful about our next steps. This may be more complex than a simple money-laundering operation."

Emily felt a chill run down her spine. Just when she thought she'd uncovered the full extent of Mark's deception, new layers were revealing themselves, each more disturbing than the last.

As she drove home, her phone buzzed with another text from Sarah:

Where are you? Stopped by your house, Claire said you went out. Everything okay?

Emily stared at the message, the familiar concern in the words now seeming sinister in light of what she'd learned. Her closest confidante was reporting her movements to her criminal husband. The people she'd trusted most were orchestrating an elaborate deception around her.

But two could play that game. If Mark and Sarah wanted to manipulate her, let them think they were succeeding. Meanwhile, she would work with Ramirez to uncover the full truth and find a way to protect herself and Claire from whatever dangerous endgame Mark was planning.

She typed a response to Sarah, her fingers steady despite the turmoil inside:

Just running errands. Coffee tomorrow still works. Looking forward to catching up.

The reply came almost instantly:

Great! Same place, 10 a.m.? Miss you! ❤

The heart emoji, once a symbol of their close friendship, now seemed like a cruel mockery. Emily put down her phone and focused on the road ahead, both literally and figuratively. The path forward was fraught with danger and uncertainty, but for the first time since this nightmare began, she had an ally she believed she could trust in Detective Ramirez.

Whatever Mark was involved in, whatever web of

deceit Sarah had helped spin around her, Emily was no longer blindly walking into their traps. Knowledge was power, and with Ramirez's help, she intended to gather enough of both to break free from Mark's control—and ensure that Claire would be protected from the fallout when his criminal empire finally came crashing down.

6

A DANGEROUS GAME ALLIES AND ADVERSARIES

Emily stared at her phone, Sarah's third **text message** of the morning glowing accusingly on the screen:

Are you coming? Been waiting 20 mins. Everything okay?

She couldn't do it. The thought of sitting across from Sarah, pretending everything was normal, while knowing her "best friend" had been reporting back to Mark, made her physically ill. Detective Ramirez had advised her to maintain normalcy, but some performances were beyond even her newfound talent for deception.

So sorry! Claire woke up sick. Need to stay home with her. Reschedule soon?

The lie came easily now, another brick in the wall she was building between her old life and whatever uncertain future awaited. Claire wasn't sick—she was at a Saturday morning debate team practice. But Sarah didn't need to know that.

Sarah's response came seconds later:

Poor thing! Need me to bring soup or meds?

The forced concern made Emily's stomach turn. How long had Sarah been playing this role? Years? Had any of their friendship been real?

No thanks, just a mild fever. Probably 24hr bug. Talk soon.

Emily set the phone down and returned to the kitchen, where Mark was reading the paper, coffee mug in hand, the picture of suburban contentment. He glanced up as she entered.

"Sarah not available?" he asked casually.

"She canceled," Emily lied, pouring herself more coffee. "Work emergency."

"Funny," Mark said, turning a page. "Thought she had Saturdays off."

Emily's pulse quickened. How did he know Sarah's schedule? Had she mentioned it, or was this another slip revealing how closely they worked together?

"Special project," she improvised. "Deadline stuff."

Mark hummed noncommittally. "Tom's covering the Preston meeting today. Poor guy's giving up his Saturday, too." He checked his watch. "Speaking of which, I should head out soon. Quarterly reports won't review themselves."

Emily's attention sharpened. "The Preston meeting? I thought that was scheduled for next week."

"It was. Client moved it up." Mark folded his newspaper. "They're meeting at that pretentious new coffee place—Onyx? Tom's probably already setting up. He likes to arrive early and stake out the good table by the windows."

Onyx had opened just last month in the trendy Westside district, all industrial chic and overpriced pour-overs. More importantly, it was public. Crowded. Safe.

"I've been wanting to try their lavender latte," Emily said, keeping her tone casual. "Maybe I'll head there after I drop off those books at the library."

Something flickered in Mark's eyes—calculation, perhaps suspicion. "I wouldn't. Place is always packed on weekends. Besides, I thought you were reorganizing the guest room today."

"Right. Maybe another time." She smiled, the muscles in her face straining with the effort.

Mark kissed her cheek before leaving, his lips cold against her skin. "Don't wait up. We're planning to get a big head start on the quarterly reviews this weekend."

The moment his car pulled away, Emily sprang into action. She had maybe thirty minutes before Tom would finish his meeting—assuming Mark's information was accurate and not some kind of trap. Her fingers trembled slightly as she texted Detective Ramirez:

Tom Mitchell at Onyx Coffee on Westside. Going to observe only. Potential chance to ID Preston client.

Ramirez had told her not to engage, just gather information. She wouldn't approach Tom—that would be reckless. But seeing who he met with, possibly photographing them together, could provide valuable intelligence for the investigation.

Emily changed quickly into jeans and a nondescript blouse, adding large sunglasses and a hat she rarely wore. The disguise wasn't elaborate, but it might prevent immediate recognition in a crowded café. She grabbed her purse and headed for the door, adrenaline already coursing through her veins.

Just as she reached for the handle, her phone buzzed with Ramirez's reply:

DO NOT approach. Surveillance only. Text location when arriving. Be careful.

Fifteen minutes later, Emily pulled into a parking space a half-block from Onyx. The café occupied the corner of a renovated brick building, its large windows offering a clear view of the interior. Perfect for people-watching—or surveillance.

She waited in her car, scanning the area for familiar faces. No sign of Frank Peterson's blue sedan, or any other neighbors' cars. Mark's car was nowhere to be seen, either. So far, so good.

Inside, Onyx was buzzing with weekend customers. Emily chose a small table near the back, partially obscured by a decorative bookshelf but with a clear sightline to the window area Mark had mentioned. She ordered a plain coffee and settled in to wait, pulse thrumming with nervous energy.

There, at the window table, Tom Mitchell sat facing a man Emily didn't recognize. Mid-fifties, silver-haired, expensive suit. They appeared deep in conversation, papers spread between them. Emily casually raised her phone, angling it to capture a photo while pretending to check messages.

The silver-haired man passed a folder to Tom, who barely glanced at its contents before tucking it into his briefcase. Money exchanged hands—not in an envelope or a check, but actual cash, discreetly slipped beneath a napkin. Tom counted it under the table, nodded once, and the conversation continued.

Emily snapped another photo, heart racing. This was exactly the kind of evidence Ramirez needed—clear documentation of suspicious financial transactions outside normal business channels.

Another figure approached their table, a woman in a cream-colored blazer. Emily nearly dropped her phone in shock.

Lisa Turner. Her neighbor.

Lisa joined the men, taking the third chair at the table. Her manner was professional and confident—nothing like the slightly awkward, overly friendly neighbor Emily knew. This Lisa moved with authority, speaking while the men listened intently.

The web of connections expanded in Emily's mind. Not just Sarah and Frank, but Lisa, too? How many people in her life were part of Mark's network?

Emily's hands trembled while she typed a quick text to Ramirez:

Tom meeting w/ older man, cash exchanged. Neighbor Lisa Turner just joined them. Taking photos.

She raised her phone again, focusing on capturing all three faces in one frame. Just as she pressed the button, Tom glanced in her direction. Their eyes met for a split second before Emily looked down at her coffee, pulse pounding in her ears.

Had he recognized her? The hat, the sunglasses, and the distance between them offered some protection, but Tom was observant. Mark had mentioned that more than once.

When she dared look up again, the three were gathering their things, conversation apparently concluded.

They stood, Tom shaking hands with the silver-haired man while Lisa checked her watch. Normal business behavior, except for the cash, the secretive manner, and the fact that Lisa Turner was supposed to be a kindergarten teacher, not whatever role she was playing here.

Emily waited until they had left the café before standing, leaving a few bills to cover her barely touched coffee. She needed to get out, report to Ramirez, and process what she'd seen.

The bright sunlight outside momentarily blinded her as she stepped onto the sidewalk. She paused, adjusting her sunglasses, planning to head straight to her car.

"Emily?"

She froze, ice flooding her veins. Slowly, she turned to face Lisa Turner, standing alone on the sidewalk, cream blazer gleaming in the sunlight.

"Lisa. Hi." Emily forced a smile. "Just grabbing coffee. You?"

Lisa's expression was unreadable. "Business meeting. I consult for a few companies on the side. Teaching doesn't pay what it used to." Her eyes flicked to Emily's hat and sunglasses. "New look?"

"Migraine day. Light sensitivity." Another lie, delivered with practiced ease.

"Shouldn't you be home with Claire? Sarah mentioned she was sick."

The trap snapped shut around her. Sarah had already

reported their canceled coffee date, and Lisa knew exactly where Emily was supposed to be.

"She's feeling better. With her father now." Emily took a step back. "I should go. Errands to run."

Lisa smiled, the expression not reaching her eyes. "Of course. Don't let me keep you." She paused, then added, "We should have you and Mark over for dinner soon. Frank's been asking about him."

"That would be lovely," Emily managed, turning toward her car, every instinct screaming at her to run.

She maintained a normal pace until she reached her vehicle, hands shaking so badly she could barely unlock the door. Once inside, she locked the doors and started the engine, checking her mirrors obsessively.

Lisa still stood on the sidewalk, phone to her ear, watching Emily's car.

Calling Mark? Tom? Reporting that Emily Johnson was where she shouldn't be, watching people she shouldn't see?

Emily pulled away from the curb, her mind racing. She couldn't go home—not yet. They would expect her there, and she needed time to think, to contact Ramirez, to process the expanding conspiracy around her.

She drove aimlessly for several blocks, constantly checking her mirrors for signs of pursuit. Nothing obvious, but that didn't mean she wasn't being followed. These people were professionals, after all.

When she felt relatively confident that no one was trailing her, Emily pulled into the parking lot of a busy shopping center and called Ramirez.

"I've been made," she said without preamble when he answered. "Lisa Turner saw me at Onyx. She knows I lied about where I was supposed to be."

"Are you safe right now?" Ramirez's voice was steady, calming.

"I think so. I'm in public, lots of people around."

"Good. Stay there. I'm sending an officer to escort you to the station. Plain clothes, unmarked car."

"Is that necessary?" Emily asked, though she already knew the answer.

"You've just observed a suspicious cash transaction involving people connected to a potential money-laundering operation, and one of those people has identified you as a witness. So, yes, I'd say it's necessary."

Put that way, the situation's gravity hit her full force. This wasn't just about uncovering Mark's secrets anymore; she had potentially placed herself in real danger.

"What about Claire?" Sudden fear gripped her. "She's at debate practice at the high school."

"I'll send another officer there. We'll bring her to the station, too, as a precaution."

"She doesn't know anything about this," Emily protested. "Mark would never hurt his own daughter."

"Probably not," Ramirez agreed. "But she could be

used as leverage against you. Better safe than sorry."

The reality of her situation crashed over Emily like a wave. In pursuing the truth, she had escalated a dangerous game, placing not just herself but Claire in potential jeopardy. How had her life unraveled so completely in just a few weeks?

"The officer will be there in ten minutes," Ramirez continued. "His name is Officer Patel. He'll identify himself with the code phrase 'Your brother sends his regards.' Don't go with anyone else, understood?"

"Understood," Emily whispered, scanning the parking lot nervously. Was that man sitting in his car watching her? Was the woman on her phone reporting her location?

"Mrs. Johnson—Emily—I know this is frightening, but you did the right thing. The information you've gathered could be crucial to our investigation."

Small comfort, Emily thought when she ended the call. She clutched her purse, containing the phone with incriminating photos. Evidence that might eventually free her from Mark's web of lies, but that now made her a threat to whatever operation he was running.

From her vantage point in the car, Emily could see most of the parking lot. Families with shopping carts, teenagers in groups, couples holding hands—normal Saturday activities unfolding in the sunlight, a sharp contrast to the shadows she now moved through.

A dark blue sedan pulled up two spaces away. The

driver—a young man in jeans and a polo shirt—surveyed the area before his gaze settled on Emily's car. He stepped out, moving casually in her direction.

Emily's hand moved to her door lock, ready to drive away, if necessary. The man approached, smiling politely.

"Mrs. Johnson? Your brother sends his regards."

Relief washed over her. "Officer Patel?"

He nodded, opening her passenger door and sliding in beside her. "Detective Ramirez sent me. We need to move quickly. I'll drive."

They switched places, and soon Emily found herself in the passenger seat as Patel navigated through Saturday traffic toward the police station.

"Another officer is picking up your daughter from the high school," he assured her. "Standard procedure, nothing to worry about."

But there was plenty to worry about. Claire would be confused, frightened. How would Emily explain any of this without revealing that her father was potentially a criminal? That their entire life had been built on deception?

"Detective Ramirez said you observed a meeting between persons of interest," Patel continued, his tone professional. "Can I see the photos you took?"

Emily hesitated. Something in his phrasing felt off. "Ramirez knows what I saw. I'll show him when we get to the station."

Patel shrugged. "Fair enough. Procedure anyway."

They drove in silence for several minutes. Emily frowned as they turned onto Wilson Avenue—this wasn't the route to the police station.

"Where are we going?" she asked, tension creeping back into her voice.

"Small detour. Avoiding traffic."

But Wilson Avenue led away from downtown, toward the industrial district. Emily's instincts screamed a warning.

"Your brother sends his regards," she said suddenly. "What's my brother's name?"

Patel's grip tightened on the steering wheel. "What?"

"If Ramirez told you to say that, he would have told you my brother's name. What is it?"

A moment of heavy silence filled the car.

"Listen, lady—"

Emily didn't wait for him to finish. She grabbed the steering wheel, jerking it sharply toward the busy intersection they were approaching. Horns blared as Patel fought for control, the car swerving wildly across lanes.

"Are you crazy?" he shouted, wrestling the wheel from her grip.

The distraction was enough. Emily unlocked her door and threw it open as the car slowed for a red light. She tumbled onto the pavement, pain shooting through her shoulder and hip, but adrenaline propelled her to her feet.

Patel was halfway out of the driver's seat, cursing as

he tried to navigate around the car to reach her. Emily ran into the intersection, weaving between stopped vehicles, ignoring the startled faces of drivers watching the scene unfold.

A city bus was just pulling away from a stop on the opposite corner. Emily sprinted toward it, waving frantically. The driver hesitated, then opened the doors. Emily scrambled aboard, fumbling for cash while the doors closed behind her.

Through the windows, she could see Patel standing in the street, phone to his ear, watching as the bus pulled away.

"You all right, miss?" the driver asked, concerned.

"Yes," Emily gasped, hand pressed to her throbbing shoulder. "Thank you for stopping."

She moved to a seat midway down the bus, her mind racing. How had they found her so quickly? How had they known which shopping center she was at? And, most terrifying of all, had the real Officer Patel reached Claire?

With trembling fingers, Emily dialed Ramirez's number.

"The officer you sent wasn't real," she said the moment he answered. "He tried to take me somewhere, not to the station. I had to jump from the car."

"What?" Ramirez's shock sounded genuine. "I haven't dispatched anyone yet. Officer Patel was still being briefed when I left to handle an emergency call."

Ice settled in Emily's veins. "Then who—"

"Where are you now?" Ramirez cut in urgently.

"On a bus. Westbound on Marshall Street."

"Stay on that bus. I'm sending a patrol car to intercept at the Riverfront stop. That's about ten minutes from your current location."

"Claire," Emily said, her voice breaking. "If they knew where I was, they might know about Claire, too."

"I've got officers heading to the high school now," Ramirez assured her. "Stay on the line with me until the patrol car reaches you."

Emily hunched in her seat, clutching the phone like a lifeline, eyes constantly scanning her fellow passengers for threats. The ordinary scene—a mother with a toddler, an elderly man reading a newspaper, teenagers with headphones—seemed surreal against the backdrop of her terror.

The bus rumbled toward Riverfront Station, each minute stretching into eternity. Emily's shoulder throbbed where she'd hit the pavement, and her mind replayed the events of the morning in a continuous loop. Lisa Turner's knowing smile. The fake Officer Patel. The almost seamless coordination of whoever was tracking her movements.

How deep did this conspiracy go? How many resources did Mark and his associates have at their disposal? The web of deception appeared increasingly vast, its strands reaching into every aspect of her life.

As the bus approached Riverfront Station, Emily spotted two police cruisers waiting, lights flashing. Relief flooded her system.

"I see the patrol cars," she told Ramirez, her voice steadier now.

"Good. Officers Chen and Rodriguez will escort you directly to me. No detours, no separate vehicles."

The bus pulled to a stop, doors hissing open. Two uniformed officers approached as Emily descended the steps, their expressions serious.

"Mrs. Johnson?" The female officer extended her badge. "Officer Chen. Detective Ramirez sent us. Are you injured?"

"My shoulder," Emily admitted. "I fell when escaping the car."

"We'll have that looked at," Chen assured her, guiding Emily toward the cruiser. "Your daughter is safe. Officers located her at the debate tournament and are bringing her to the station now."

The simple sentence—"Your daughter is safe"—nearly broke Emily's composure. She hadn't realized how terrified she'd been for Claire until that moment.

As they drove toward the station, Emily stared out the window at the familiar streets of the city she'd called home for fifteen years. The shops she frequented, the park where Claire had learned how to ride a bike, the restaurants where she and Mark had celebrated anniversaries—all unchanged, yet fundamentally altered by her perception.

Somewhere in this normal-seeming community, her husband operated a criminal enterprise sophisticated enough to deploy fake police officers within minutes of identifying a threat. People she had trusted—Sarah, Lisa, perhaps even David—were part of an elaborate network designed to protect Mark's secrets. And she, through her determination to uncover the truth, had placed herself and Claire directly in their crosshairs.

The game had escalated beyond investigation into something far more dangerous. No longer was Emily simply seeking answers; she was fighting for her safety and her daughter's future. When the police station came into view, Emily steeled herself for whatever came next, knowing only one thing with certainty: There was no going back to the life she had known.

7

THE TRUTH REVEALED?

The police station conference room felt **sterile and cold**, its institutional furniture and fluorescent lighting a stark contrast to the emotional turmoil raging inside Emily. Claire sat beside her, confusion and fear etched across her young face. Detective Ramirez had explained the situation earlier in the vaguest terms possible—a potential threat related to Emily's "ongoing cooperation with an investigation"—but Claire was perceptive enough to know something more significant was happening.

"Mom, please," Claire whispered, her voice trembling. "What's really going on? Why did police officers pull me out of debate practice?"

Before Emily could formulate a response that wouldn't shatter their world entirely, the conference room door swung open. Mark stood in the doorway, Detective Ramirez just behind him, tension radiating between the two men.

"Daddy!" Claire jumped up, relief flooding her features.

Mark embraced their daughter, eyes locked on Emily over Claire's shoulder. His expression was unreadable—concern, anger, perhaps even fear—all carefully masked behind the facade of a worried father.

"Are you okay, sweetheart?" he asked Claire, his voice gentler than Emily had heard it in weeks.

"I'm fine, just confused." Claire pulled back, looking between her parents. "No one will tell me what's going on."

Mark turned to Ramirez. "May I have a moment with my family, Detective?"

Ramirez hesitated, glancing at Emily with clear concern. "Mrs. Johnson?"

Emily felt trapped between impossible choices. Refusing would only heighten Claire's anxiety and potentially reveal more than she was ready to explain. But agreeing meant facing Mark without the buffer of law enforcement—facing a man she now knew was capable of elaborate deception and possibly much worse.

"It's fine," she said finally, the words feeling like a surrender.

Ramirez nodded reluctantly. "I'll be right outside. Mrs. Johnson. Remember what we discussed." The pointed reminder of their safety plan hung in the air as he exited, closing the door with a soft click.

The moment they were alone, Mark's demeanor shifted—subtle but unmistakable. His posture straightened, eyes hardening even as his voice remained gentle.

"Claire, sweetheart, there's been a misunderstanding," he began, guiding their daughter back to her chair. "Your mother's been under a lot of stress lately. Work pressure, migraines—you've noticed, right?"

Claire nodded uncertainly, glancing at Emily.

"She saw something today that she misinterpreted, and in her confusion, she contacted the police." Mark sighed, the picture of a concerned husband. "It's created quite a situation, but everything's going to be fine now."

"That's not what happened," Emily interjected, anger flaring. "Claire, your father is—"

"Emily." Mark's voice sharpened momentarily before softening again. "Let's not make this more upsetting for Claire than it already is."

The familiar pattern—Mark controlling the narrative, subtly undermining her—was so practiced that Claire seemed to accept it without question. The realization broke

Emily's heart. How many times had she watched this dynamic play out without recognizing it for what it was?

"Can we go home now?" Claire asked, the plaintive question of a child who simply wanted normalcy restored.

Mark smiled reassuringly. "That's exactly what we're going to do. I've spoken with Detective Ramirez and cleared everything up."

"You haven't cleared anything," Emily said, struggling to keep her voice steady. "They've been tracking your financial transactions for weeks. They know about Tom Mitchell, about the storage unit—"

"Mom, please stop," Claire interrupted, tears forming. "You're scaring me."

Mark placed a protective arm around their daughter. "It's okay, Claire. Mom's just confused." To Emily, his expression hardened almost imperceptibly. "The detective understands now that this is all a terrible misunderstanding. They have no evidence of any wrongdoing because there is none. Ramirez can't legally hold any of us."

The worst part was that Mark was right. Despite her discoveries, despite the fake police officer who had tried to abduct her, there wasn't yet enough concrete evidence to arrest Mark. The photos from the coffee shop showed suspicious behavior, but nothing overtly illegal. The storage unit was rented in Mark's name, and he had every right to store private financial documents. Even the incident with the fake officer couldn't be directly linked to Mark without further investigation.

Ramirez had explained it all while the doctor examined Emily's bruised shoulder. They needed more time to build a case—bank records, witness statements, documentary evidence of laundered funds. Meanwhile, Mark remained free, and as Claire's father, he had every legal right to take her home.

"Claire needs to come home with me," Emily insisted, a last desperate attempt to protect her daughter.

"With us," Mark corrected smoothly. "We're still a family, Emily. Whatever you think you've discovered, whatever paranoid theories you've developed, we can work through this together." He turned to Claire. "Right, sweetheart? We all belong at home together."

Claire nodded eagerly, clearly relieved at this apparent resolution. "Please, Mom. Let's just go home."

Emily felt the trap closing around her. If she refused to return home, she would have to explain everything to Claire immediately, here in this sterile police station, without preparation or support. If she went home with Mark, she would be walking back into the lion's den—but she would be with Claire, able to protect her directly.

The decision crystallized with painful clarity. "Fine. We'll all go home. Together."

Mark's smile didn't reach his eyes. "Perfect. I've already spoken with Ramirez. He understands this is a family matter now."

When Detective Ramirez re-entered, his expression confirmed Emily's fears. Without sufficient evidence for an arrest, he couldn't legally prevent Mark from taking his family home. The best he could offer was a patrol car driving by the house periodically through the night.

"Mrs. Johnson, are you sure about this?" Ramirez asked quietly as they prepared to leave.

She nodded, slipping the detective's card deeper into her pocket. "I need to be with my daughter."

"Call immediately if anything concerns you," he murmured. "And remember: We're making progress on those financial records. This is temporary."

The drive home unfolded in uncomfortable silence, Claire sitting in the back seat of Mark's car while Emily stared out the passenger window, mind racing through scenarios and escape plans. Mark maintained a perfect facade of normalcy, commenting on weekend traffic and asking Claire about her debate tournament as if nothing extraordinary had happened.

They arrived home, so familiar and beautiful on the outside, but hiding dark secrets within. Emily stepped through the front door with the caution of someone entering enemy territory.

"Claire, why don't you go upstairs and rest?" Mark suggested. "It's been a stressful day for everyone."

"I'm not tired," Claire protested. "And I still don't understand what's happening."

"Your mother and I need to talk privately," Mark insisted, his tone gentle but firm. "We'll explain everything later, I promise."

Claire hesitated, looking to Emily for confirmation.

"It's okay," Emily assured her, though nothing felt further from the truth. "We do need to talk. I'll come check on you afterward."

After Claire reluctantly climbed the stairs, silence fell between Emily and Mark. He moved to the kitchen, his actions deliberately casual as he opened the refrigerator.

"Wine?" he offered, as if this were any normal evening.

"Stop it," Emily said, her voice low but intense. "Stop pretending this is normal."

Mark set down the wine bottle, something shifting in his demeanor. The pleasant mask slipped, revealing a colder calculation beneath.

"Let's talk in the living room," he said, not a suggestion but a command.

Emily followed, hyperaware of every movement, every sound in the house. The living room—where they'd watched movies as a family, celebrated birthdays, built their life together—now felt like an interrogation chamber.

She didn't sit. Neither did Mark. They faced each other like combatants assessing their opponent's weaknesses.

"I know everything," Emily said, drawing strength from the simple truth. "The money laundering through

Preston Financial. The coded ledgers using our family names. The blackmail materials in your storage unit. Tom Mitchell and your other associates."

Mark's expression remained carefully neutral. "What exactly do you think you know, Emily?"

"Don't." She held up a hand. "Don't insult me by denying it. I found the storage unit. I saw the documents. I've photographed everything."

A flicker of something—concern, perhaps even fear— crossed Mark's face before he controlled it. "And you've shared these... theories with the police?"

"With Detective Ramirez, yes. He's building a case."

Mark sighed, running a hand through his hair in a gesture that once seemed endearing but now struck Emily as calculated. "Emily, listen to yourself. You're talking about your husband of fifteen years like he's some kind of criminal mastermind."

"I'm talking about the evidence I found with my own eyes," she countered. "Explain the storage unit. Explain the surveillance photos of me and Claire labeled 'insurance.' Explain the cash exchanges I witnessed today between Tom and your clients."

Mark's eyes narrowed at the last revelation. "You were following Tom?"

"Answer my questions," Emily insisted.

For a moment, Mark seemed to consider his options. Then his approach shifted entirely. He walked over to the bookshelf, pulling out a thick folder she hadn't seen before.

"You want answers? Fine. Let's look at what you think you've found."

He opened the folder, spreading documents across the coffee table. Emily recognized them immediately—photocopies of the ledgers she'd discovered in the storage unit. But as she looked closer, she realized something was wrong. The figures were different. The codes she remembered so clearly were altered or missing entirely.

"These are standard investment portfolios," Mark explained, his voice taking on the patient tone he used when explaining financial concepts to clients. "Yes, they include code names for client privacy—standard practice in our industry. Johnson-Reynolds refers to the Johnson Reynolds Fund, a perfectly legitimate investment vehicle we offer high-net-worth clients."

Emily shook her head. "No, that's not what I saw. The documents listed illegal transfers, money being 'cleaned'—"

"Is that what you saw? Or what you think you saw?" Mark's voice softened with concern. "Emily, you've been under tremendous stress. Working too hard, sleeping poorly. Remember those migraines last month? The doctor mentioned they could cause memory issues, even paranoia in extreme cases."

"Don't try to gaslight me," Emily snapped, though doubt began creeping in at the edges of her certainty. The documents before her looked official, legitimate—different from what she remembered photographing.

"I'm trying to help you," Mark insisted. "These conspiracy theories, these accusations—they're not just harmful to me; they're dangerous for our family. Think about Claire."

"I *am* thinking about Claire!" Emily's voice rose despite her efforts to control it. "I'm trying to protect her from whatever criminal enterprise you're running!"

Mark's expression darkened momentarily before he visibly composed himself. "Emily, this has gone far enough. Yes, I have private financial documents in a storage unit. Yes, I use code names for clients. Yes, I sometimes meet associates outside the office. None of that is illegal."

"What about the surveillance photos of me and Claire?"

Mark sighed heavily, reaching for another folder. "You mean these?"

He spread several photos on the table. They showed Emily and Claire at the mall, similar to what she'd seen in the storage unit, but these were clearly printed from their family cloud account. Normal family photos she herself had taken or appeared in.

"I was pulling together pictures for Claire's graduation slideshow," Mark explained. "It was supposed to be a surprise."

Doubt gnawed at Emily's certainty. Had she misinterpreted innocent photos? Had the stress and suspicion warped her perception?

No. She remembered clearly what she'd seen. The photos in the storage unit had been surveillance images, not family photos. The ledgers had documented illegal activities, not legitimate investments.

"You're manipulating evidence," she accused. "These aren't what I found in the storage unit."

"Emily, listen to yourself," Mark said, concern etched across his features. "You break into my private storage unit, misinterpret normal business documents, and construct an elaborate conspiracy theory. Now, when I show you the actual documents, you accuse me of manipulation?"

Put that way, her allegations sounded paranoid, even delusional. Emily felt her resolve wavering, doubt seeping in like poison.

"What about Sarah?" she demanded, changing tactics. "And Lisa Turner? I saw her meeting with Tom today, exchanging documents and cash. Explain that."

Something flickered in Mark's eyes—surprise, perhaps, that she knew about Lisa. "Sarah has nothing to do with any of this," he said firmly. "As for Lisa—yes, she consults for some of our clients. She had a background in finance before she became a teacher. The cash you saw was probably a refund for expenses. Everything has a simple explanation if you're willing to hear it."

"And the fake police officer who tried to abduct me today? Was that a 'simple explanation,' too?"

Mark's calm smile cracked slightly, genuine confusion crossing his features. "What fake officer? Emily, what are you talking about?"

Either he was an exceptional actor, or he genuinely didn't know about the attempted abduction. Could there be elements of this conspiracy that Mark himself wasn't aware of? Players working against him or without his knowledge?

Before she could pursue this line of questioning, footsteps on the stairs announced Claire's presence. She appeared in the doorway, eyes red from crying.

"I can hear you fighting from upstairs," she said, voice small and hurt. "Please stop."

Mark immediately shifted into concerned father mode, walking across the room to Claire and placing an arm around her shoulders. "We're not fighting, sweetheart. Just having an important conversation."

Claire looked at the documents spread across the coffee table. "What's all this?"

"Nothing important," Mark assured her. "Just some work things your mother had questions about."

Emily watched this performance with new eyes, seeing how effortlessly Mark controlled narratives, shifted between roles, and manipulated perceptions. Even now, knowing what she knew, she found herself half-convinced by his explanations, his seemingly reasonable answers.

"Claire, your father and I need to finish our discussion," Emily said carefully. "It's important. Can you give us a little more time?"

Claire hesitated, looking between them. "Are you getting divorced?" The direct question, delivered with teenage bluntness, hung in the air between them.

"No, of course not," Mark answered quickly. "Every marriage has rough patches. We're working through some misunderstandings, that's all."

Emily said nothing, unable to offer false reassurances but unwilling to shatter her daughter's world without preparation.

"Go back upstairs, Claire," Mark said gently. "Maybe put on those noise-canceling headphones I got you. Your mother and I will come talk to you together when we're done."

After Claire reluctantly retreated, Mark's demeanor changed yet again. The gentle father vanished, replaced by something harder, more desperate.

"Do you have any idea what you're doing?" he asked, voice low and intense. "The people Tom works with—they don't tolerate loose ends or liabilities. By going to the police, you've put yourself in danger. Put Claire in danger."

"So, you admit there's something criminal happening," Emily seized on his implicit statement.

Mark closed his eyes briefly, as if gathering himself. When he opened them, Emily was shocked to see tears forming.

"You want the truth?" His voice cracked slightly. "The truth is I'm terrified. Tom Mitchell isn't who you think—who I thought—he was. The firm has been under tremendous pressure. Some of our clients... they have expectations that aren't always strictly by the book."

"You're saying Tom is involved in criminal activity, but you're not?" Emily's disbelief was evident in her tone.

"I'm saying I've been naive," Mark said, a tear escaping down his cheek. "I've been trying to protect the firm, protect our clients, and make enough money to secure our future. But Tom's been taking things too far. The storage unit—those documents—they're my insurance. Evidence I've been gathering."

"Evidence of what, exactly?"

"Tom's been pressuring me to sign off on transactions I'm not comfortable with. Using my connections, my client relationships." Mark ran his hands through his hair, looking genuinely distressed. "When I started pushing back, things got... complicated. Lisa's been helping me track some of the money flows. I needed records somewhere secure, away from the office."

Emily stared at him, trying to process this new narrative. It neatly explained the storage unit, the suspicious documents, even Lisa's involvement—all while positioning Mark as a victim rather than the perpetrator. It was either the truth or an incredibly calculated deception.

"And the surveillance photos of me and Claire? The ones labeled 'insurance'?"

Mark looked confused. "Are you talking about the family photos I've been gathering for Claire's graduation? They were mixed in with the financial documents."

"No," Emily insisted, though doubt began to creep in. "These were surveillance photos. They had dates and locations stamped on them."

"Metadata from our cloud account, probably," Mark suggested. "Emily, I've been under incredible stress. Tom's been making threats, implying he has connections that could hurt us. But I would never, ever risk you or Claire."

"Then who sent the fake officer today?" Emily demanded. "Who tried to have me abducted?"

Mark's confusion seemed genuine. "I still don't know what you are talking about."

"Someone posed as an officer Ramirez supposedly sent. They tried to take me somewhere—not to the station."

Mark's face paled. "My God. That... that has to be Tom. He must have found out you were watching him today." He moved closer, his expression suddenly urgent. "Emily, this is exactly what I've been afraid of. Tom's got connections—dangerous people. This is why you need to drop this investigation. Tell Ramirez you made a mistake."

"So I should just ignore everything I've seen? Pretend none of this is happening?"

"You don't understand what we're dealing with,"

Mark insisted, his voice breaking. "These people—they don't play by normal rules. If they think you're a threat... I've been trying to find a way out, to gather enough evidence against Tom without exposing our family to danger."

"Why didn't you go to the police yourself?" Emily challenged.

"With what? Suspicions? Transactions that I technically approved? I needed proof that I was being coerced." Mark stepped closer, taking her hands in his before she could pull away. "Emily, please. Fifteen years together. A family. A life. Don't throw it away before I can explain everything properly. Let me show you what I've been gathering, make you understand."

His touch, once so familiar and comforting, now felt like another manipulation. Yet the desperation in his eyes seemed real—the first genuine emotion she'd seen from him in weeks.

"If what you're saying is true," Emily said quietly, "then come with me to Detective Ramirez. Show him what you've found on Tom. Explain the situation."

Mark's expression hardened. "That's not an option. Not yet. I don't have enough evidence to protect myself. If Tom finds out I've spoken to the police, we all become targets. The only way forward is carefully, methodically building a case while keeping our family safe."

"A case built on more secrets and lies," Emily

countered.

"On survival," Mark corrected, his grip on her hands tightening slightly. "Emily, I'm begging you. For Claire's sake, if not for mine—give me time to prove what I'm telling you."

Mark seemed to sense her wavering resolve. He pulled her closer, wrapping his arms around her in an embrace that felt both familiar and utterly foreign.

"I love you," he whispered, his voice breaking. "I've made mistakes, trusted the wrong people, but that has never changed. Give me a chance to fix this."

Emily stood rigid in his embrace, mind racing. Was any part of this genuine? The tears, the explanation that positioned Tom as the villain, the apparent fear for their safety—were they real emotions or another calculated performance? She could no longer distinguish Mark's truth from his lies.

"I need time to think," she said finally, extracting herself from his arms. "No more discussions tonight. No more explanations or justifications."

Mark nodded, wiping away tears with the back of his hand. "Of course. Whatever you need."

As Emily turned to leave the room, he called after her softly.

"Emily? Where will you sleep tonight?"

The question carried implications she wasn't ready to face—the future of their marriage, the immediate safety concerns, the practical reality of continuing to share a home with a man she now feared and mistrusted.

"In the guest room," she answered, not looking back. "And Mark? I'm locking the door."

His silence followed her up the stairs as she checked on Claire, finding her finally asleep with headphones on, then retreated to the guest bedroom. Emily turned the lock, then pushed a chair under the doorknob for good measure. She sat on the edge of the bed, physically and emotionally exhausted but too wired for sleep.

Her phone buzzed with a text from Ramirez:

Patrol car stationed nearby. Call if needed. Making progress on financial records.

Small comfort as she sat alone in a locked room, separated from her sleeping daughter by a hallway that had never seemed so long. Mark's tearful confession replayed in her mind, alongside his skilled manipulation of documents and narrative. The doubts he'd planted took root despite her efforts to maintain clarity.

Had she misinterpreted innocent business practices? Was Mark truly being pressured by Tom and gathering evidence to protect himself? Or was this exactly what Mark wanted her to think—to doubt herself, question her memory, and retreat from her accusations?

The contradictions and inconsistencies swirled in her mind. If the storage unit contained Mark's evidence against Tom, why had he kept it secret from her? If he was truly worried about their safety, why didn't he mention it until he was confronted? And what about Sarah—was she helping Mark against Tom, or helping Tom against Mark, or involved in some other way entirely?

The truth and lies had become so intertwined that separating them felt impossible. Only one thing remained clear: Somewhere in this house, her daughter slept peacefully, unaware that her world balanced on a knife's edge between devastating truth and comforting deception.

Emily moved to the window, looking out at the quiet street below. A police cruiser was parked at the corner, its presence both reassuring and a stark reminder of the danger surrounding them. The familiar houses of their neighbors—Frank Peterson's blue shutters, the Millers' perfectly maintained lawn, Lisa Turner's garden—now seemed like facades hiding unknown threats.

Whom could she trust? How many of these seemingly ordinary people were part of Mark's network? And, most troubling of all—what would happen when morning came, forcing her to make decisions that would irrevocably alter Claire's life?

Emily leaned her forehead against the cool glass, her tears finally flowing freely. Tomorrow would bring difficult conversations, impossible choices, and dangers she couldn't yet fully comprehend. But tonight, locked in this guest room with her thoughts, Emily mourned the death of her marriage and the life she'd believed was real.

8

TIES THAT BIND

Morning light filtered through the **guest room** blinds, finding Emily already awake, sitting on the edge of the bed. She hadn't slept more than fitful snatches throughout the night, her mind endlessly replaying Mark's tearful explanation and her own doubts. Was Tom Mitchell truly the villain in this scenario, with Mark merely a reluctant participant? Or was Mark masterfully manipulating her emotions, creating an elaborate alternate narrative to explain away the evidence?

The soft ping of her phone drew her attention. Another text from Sarah:

We need to talk. Alone. It's important. Coffee at my place? 10 a.m.?

Emily stared at the message, conflicted. After what Ramirez had shown her—Sarah meeting with Tom, entering Frank Peterson's house where Mark later joined her—she couldn't trust Sarah. Yet, confronting her might yield answers that continued evasion would not.

Okay. See you at 10.

She dressed quietly, listening for movement in the house. Claire's door remained closed—sleeping in on a Sunday, as usual. From downstairs came the faint sounds of Mark in the kitchen. Coffee brewing. Cupboards opening and closing.

Emily took a deep breath and descended the stairs, steeling herself for the performance ahead.

Mark looked up as she entered the kitchen, his expression a mixture of concern and wariness. Dark circles underlined his eyes, suggesting his night had been as sleepless as hers.

"Morning," he offered cautiously, holding out a mug of coffee prepared exactly as she liked it. "How did you sleep?"

"Fine," Emily lied, accepting the coffee but maintaining distance between them. "I'm going to Sarah's this morning."

Something flickered in Mark's eyes—alarm? Calculation? "Is that a good idea? After everything we discussed last night—"

"I need space to think," Emily cut him off. "And I need to talk to Sarah."

"About what happened at the police station?" Mark kept his voice low, glancing toward the stairs that led to Claire's room.

"About everything." Emily met his gaze steadily. "Unless there's some reason you don't want me talking to Sarah?"

Mark hesitated, seeming to choose his words carefully. "I'm just concerned about your safety. If Tom is monitoring our movements—"

"I'll be fine." Emily sipped her coffee, watching Mark over the rim of her mug. "Sarah's been my friend for twenty years."

"Of course," Mark conceded with a tight smile. "Will you be back for lunch? Claire mentioned wanting to try that new Thai place."

The casual domestic planning felt surreal against the backdrop of criminal investigations and suspected betrayals. "I don't know how long I'll be."

Mark nodded, disappointment evident in his posture. "Emily, about last night—"

"Not now," she interrupted. "I told you I need time to

process everything."

"Right." He set down his coffee mug. "Just... be careful."

The concern in his voice sounded genuine, which only deepened Emily's confusion. If Mark was telling the truth about Tom being the real threat, then his worry was justified. If he was lying, then his performance was masterful.

She left the house thirty minutes later, checking her rearview mirror consistently for any sign of being followed. Detective Ramirez had advised her to maintain normal routines while they built their case, but nothing felt normal anymore. Every neighbor walking their dog, every car that lingered too long at a stop sign, every casual greeting called across lawns—all triggered warnings in her heightened state of vigilance.

Sarah's modest craftsman-style home looked exactly as it always had—welcoming flower boxes, cheerful yellow door, and wind chimes tinkling gently on the front porch— yet Emily approached with the caution of someone entering enemy territory, her purse clutched close, her phone primed to dial Ramirez, if necessary.

Before she could knock, the door swung open. Sarah stood in the entryway, her usual warm smile replaced by an expression of wary determination.

"Come in quickly," she said, glancing past Emily at the street beyond. "Were you followed?"

The question, matching Emily's paranoia, caught her off guard. "I don't think so. Why would I be?"

Sarah closed and locked the door behind them, then drew the living room blinds before turning to face Emily. "Because we're both in danger, and we need to talk."

Emily remained standing, maintaining distance between them. "I saw you, Sarah. With Tom Mitchell at The Grand Hotel. And then at Frank Peterson's house with Mark."

Sarah's shoulders slumped slightly. "I know. Ramirez showed you the surveillance footage."

"So, you admit it?" Emily felt anger rising, despite her determination to remain calm. "You've been working with them all along?"

"No. I mean, yes, but not how you think." Sarah gestured toward the dining room. "Please, sit down. I have something to show you."

Emily hesitated, then followed Sarah to the dining table, which was covered with files, photographs, and what appeared to be financial records.

"What is all this?"

Sarah took a deep breath. "My investigation into Preston Financial and Tom Mitchell. Going back eighteen months."

Emily stared at the documents, struggling to process this new twist. "Your investigation? I don't understand."

"You remember what I did when I lived in Chicago for

four years?" Sarah began, pulling out a chair for Emily. "It was not just your average newspaper articles. I was an investigative reporter for the Chicago *Tribune*, specializing in financial crimes. I came home after receiving threats related to a story I was working on—a money-laundering operation tied to several investment firms, including a smaller branch of Preston Financial."

Emily sank into the chair, her mind racing to adjust this new information against everything she thought she knew.

"When I moved back home to start over, I had no idea Mark worked for Preston's main office. It wasn't until your holiday party three years ago, when I overheard him mentioning some clients I recognized from my investigation, that I began to suspect he might be involved."

"Three years?" Emily's voice rose in disbelief. "You've suspected Mark for three years and never said anything?"

Sarah shook her head. "I didn't suspect Mark specifically—I suspected Preston Financial was continuing the practices I'd been investigating in Chicago. I had no evidence Mark was personally involved. In fact, until recently, I believed he might be an unwitting participant."

"And now?"

Sarah hesitated. "Now I don't know. Tom Mitchell is definitely dirty—I've tracked millions moving through accounts he manages. But Mark's role has been harder to determine. He's either very careful or genuinely peripheral."

Emily's head swam with this revelation. Her closest friend, her confidante through marital troubles and parenting challenges, had been secretly investigating her husband for years.

"The coffee shop conversations," Emily realized suddenly. "All those times I vented about Mark working late, missing family events, being secretive about finances—you were gathering information."

"Not at first," Sarah insisted, her expression pained. "Our friendship is real, Emily. I never intended to use you as a source. But when you started noticing discrepancies yourself, sharing concerns about Mark's behavior, I couldn't ignore the patterns."

Emily felt sick. "So, when I first told you about finding that text message, about my suspicions, you already had your own investigation underway."

"Yes." Sarah met her gaze directly. "And I encouraged you to look deeper because I thought you deserved the truth, whatever it was."

"The cameras you gave me—were those just to gather evidence for your story?"

"No. They were genuinely for your protection. By that point, I was concerned that if Mark was involved and realized you were suspicious, you could be in danger."

Emily's mind raced through every conversation they'd

shared in recent weeks, reframing them in light of these revelations. "And meeting Tom Mitchell? How do you explain that?"

Sarah pulled a small recording device from among the papers. "I've been working to turn him into a source. Pretending to be a potential investor with family money to move discreetly. The meeting you saw was our third. I was wearing a wire."

She pressed play, and Tom's voice emerged from the small speaker:

"—can definitely help with the offshore structuring. Our fee is higher than standard wealth management, but the privacy benefits more than compensate—"

Sarah stopped the recording. "I've been gathering evidence on Tom for months. The meetings at Frank Peterson's house were similar—Frank isn't involved in the criminal side, but he's a former banking executive with connections I needed."

"And Mark? Why was he at Peterson's house that day?"

Sarah's expression grew more guarded. "That's... complicated. Frank has been helping me understand some of the more technical aspects of the transactions I've uncovered. He reached out to Mark with questions, under the guise of seeking investment advice for his nephew. I didn't know Mark would be there that day."

Emily studied her friend's face, searching for signs of

deception. Either Sarah was telling the truth about conducting her own investigation, or this was an incredibly elaborate cover story.

"Why didn't you tell me any of this?" Emily asked, the hurt evident in her voice.

"Journalistic ethics initially. Then, when you began your own investigation, I worried about compromising mine. And honestly, Emily, I wasn't sure how you'd react to learning your closest friend had been investigating your husband." Sarah's eyes were apologetic but resolute. "Besides, I wasn't certain of Mark's involvement until very recently. I didn't want to destroy your marriage based on suspicion."

"So what changed? Why tell me now?"

"Because things have escalated dangerously." Sarah pulled a file from the stack. "Two days ago, one of my sources inside Preston Financial was found dead in his apartment. Apparent suicide, but I don't believe it for a second. I've realized that keeping you in the dark is putting you at risk.

She opened the file, revealing photos of a middle-aged man Emily vaguely recognized from Mark's company parties. "Jeffrey Winters. Accounting department. He'd been feeding me information about irregular transactions. The day before he died, he told me he'd found something big—something that implicated senior management."

Emily felt a chill. "I remember Jeff. He asked about a

'cabin weekend,' and Mark shut down the conversation."

Sarah nodded grimly. "Jeff had been tracking a pattern of cash deposits linked to code names. Johnson-Reynolds was one of them."

"Mark claims Tom is the one running the operation, that he's been gathering evidence against Tom in that storage unit."

Sarah considered this. "It's possible, I suppose. The evidence I've gathered definitely points to Tom as a major player. But someone at Mark's level would have to be involved in approving the suspicious transactions."

"Unless he was being coerced or manipulated, like he claims."

"You believe him?" Sarah asked carefully.

Emily sighed. "I don't know what to believe anymore. Last night, Mark seemed genuinely terrified—for himself, for me, for Claire. Either he's being honest about being caught in something he can't control, or he's the most convincing liar I've ever met."

Sarah reached across the table, hesitating before resting her hand on Emily's. "I'm so sorry, Em. I never wanted to be in this position—investigating your husband, keeping secrets from you. Our friendship has always been real, even when I couldn't tell you everything."

Emily didn't pull away, but neither did she return the gesture of affection. "If what you're saying is true, you've been using our friendship to gather information for years."

"Not using," Sarah corrected gently. "Compartmentalizing. Being your friend while also following leads that sometimes involved your husband's firm. I never fabricated conversations or manipulated you for information."

A memory surfaced in Emily's mind. "The cameras you gave me—you said they were your ex's. That was a lie."

Sarah had the grace to look sheepish. "A small one. They were actually from my investigative kit."

"And all those times you encouraged me to dig deeper into Mark's behavior?"

"I genuinely believed you deserved the truth. And yes, I hoped your discoveries might confirm or disprove my suspicions about Mark's involvement."

Emily stood abruptly, needing space. She moved to Sarah's kitchen window, looking out at the peaceful backyard that seemed a world away from money laundering, fake police officers, and friends with hidden agendas.

"Does Ramirez know about your investigation?" she asked without turning around.

"Not everything. I approached him six weeks ago with some preliminary evidence about Preston Financial. He's been cautious—freelance journalists don't always make credible witnesses in financial crime cases. When you went to him independently, it strengthened my claims."

Emily turned to face her friend. "So, where does this leave us? I have a husband who may or may not be involved in criminal activity, and a best friend who's been investigating him behind my back for years. Who exactly am I supposed to trust?"

"Trust the evidence," Sarah said simply. "Not Mark's explanations or my theories—the concrete evidence we both find. Between your discoveries and my investigation, we can piece together the truth."

A cynical laugh escaped Emily. "The evidence changes depending on who's presenting it. Mark showed me altered versions of the documents I found in the storage unit—same format, different content. If I can't trust what I see with my own eyes, how can I trust anything?"

Sarah's expression grew more determined. "Then we need to get indisputable evidence. Banking records that can't be altered. Witness testimony. Recordings like the ones I've made of Tom."

"And if that evidence confirms Mark's involvement? What then? Do I become a source in your exposé? The devastated wife quoted in your story about suburban money laundering?"

The bitter words hung between them, heavy with Emily's sense of betrayal.

"This was never about a story for me," Sarah said quietly. "Not since I realized you and Claire might be affected. This is about justice and your safety. If Mark is involved, he's tangled with dangerous people who've already killed once to protect their operation."

Emily's anger deflated slightly, replaced by the same weariness that had plagued her for weeks. "I don't even know who to believe anymore. Mark tells me Tom is the criminal, forcing him to participate. You tell me you're investigating them both while pretending to be my friend. Detective Ramirez shows me footage of you with Tom that suggests you're working together. Every time I think I understand what's happening, the story changes."

"I know it's overwhelming," Sarah acknowledged. "But we need to focus on protecting you and Claire right now. Everything else—my investigation, Mark's claims, even our friendship—can be sorted out later."

Emily considered this. Whatever Sarah's motivations, her concern for their safety seemed genuine. And with Claire caught in the middle of this expanding web of deception, Emily needed allies wherever she could find them.

"Mark mentioned Lisa Turner is helping him track the money," Emily said, watching for Sarah's reaction.

Surprise flickered across Sarah's features. "Lisa? The kindergarten teacher? That's... unexpected."

"I saw her meeting with Tom yesterday, at Onyx Coffee. She said she 'consults for companies on the side.'"

Sarah frowned, making notes. "I've never connected Lisa to any of this. That's concerning. It suggests the network is larger than I realized."

Emily hesitated, then asked the question that had been haunting her. "Sarah, do you think Claire and I are in immediate danger?"

Sarah set down her pen, meeting Emily's gaze directly. "I think if Mark is involved and realizes you're gathering evidence against him, yes. If he's telling the truth about being pressured by Tom, then the danger comes from Tom's associates discovering Mark's evidence gathering."

"Either way, not a great situation," Emily observed grimly.

"No," Sarah agreed. "Which is why I think you and Claire should stay somewhere else for a while. Not here—my place is too obvious—but somewhere Mark wouldn't immediately look."

Emily shook her head. "I can't just disappear with Claire. She has school and activities. And Mark has legal rights as her father. If I take her without evidence of danger, it could backfire in a custody situation."

"Then let me help you get concrete evidence," Sarah urged. "Something undeniable that will protect you legally if you need to leave."

Emily studied her friend—or the woman she had believed was her friend. Sarah's investigation complicated everything, adding another layer of potential deception to a situation already mired in lies. Yet her expertise in financial investigations could be valuable in uncovering the truth.

"What exactly are you proposing?" Emily asked cautiously.

"We combine our evidence. Work with Ramirez to build a solid case. I have recordings of Tom discussing illegal financial arrangements. You have photos from the storage unit. Together, it might be enough for warrants or formal surveillance."

"And our friendship?"

Sarah's expression softened with genuine pain. "All of it was real, Emily. I compartmentalized my investigation, but I never manufactured our connection. You've been the most important person in my life since college. That's why this has been so difficult—watching you potentially married to someone involved in the same criminal activities that drove me from my career and home in Chicago."

Before Emily could respond, her phone buzzed with a text from Mark:

Where are you? Thought you'd be back by now. Claire's asking about lunch plans.

The ordinary domestic message felt jarring against the backdrop of their conversation about money laundering and potential danger. It was a reminder of how quickly her normal life had dissolved into this nightmare of suspicion and fear.

"I should go," Emily said, rising. "Claire's waiting for me."

"Emily, please be careful," Sarah urged. "Whether

Mark is a victim or a perpetrator, the people behind these operations are dangerous. Promise me you won't confront him with anything we've discussed."

Emily gathered her purse, suddenly exhausted by the weight of secrets and counterclaims. "I've gotten quite good at hiding my thoughts from my husband lately."

She paused at the door. "I'll talk to Ramirez tomorrow. Tell him about your investigation, suggest combining our evidence. But Sarah? I'm not doing this for you or your story. I'm doing it for Claire. To keep her safe and to figure out what kind of father she actually has."

Sarah nodded, understanding the boundaries being established. "That's all I'm asking."

As Emily drove home, her mind sorted through the new information, trying to find a solid foundation of truth amid the shifting narratives. If Sarah really was an investigative journalist tracking a money-laundering operation, her suspicious behavior made sense. The meetings with Tom, the interest in Mark's work, the surveillance equipment—all would be part of her investigation.

But why hide it for so long? Why encourage Emily to investigate her own husband without revealing the larger context? And, most troublingly, why had Detective Ramirez presented the surveillance footage as evidence of Sarah's potential complicity rather than explaining her role as an informant?

Unless Ramirez didn't know. Or didn't believe Sarah's claims about being a journalist. Or was he compromised in some way?

The endless possibilities and contradictions made Emily's head throb. Every person in her life now existed in a quantum state of potential trustworthiness and betrayal—Mark, Sarah, Lisa, David, even Ramirez. The only person she could trust unreservedly was Claire, the innocent caught in this web of adult deception.

As she pulled into her driveway, Emily made a decision. Whatever the truth about Mark and Sarah might be, her priority had to be protecting Claire. That meant gathering incontrovertible evidence, creating a safety plan, and preparing for any eventuality—even the possibility that her fifteen-year marriage and twenty-year friendship were both built on foundations of lies.

Mark opened the front door as she approached, Claire visible behind him, phone in hand, oblivious to the momentous shifts occurring in her family's reality.

"Everything okay with Sarah?" Mark asked, his tone casual but his eyes watchful.

Emily managed a faint smile. "Fine. Just catching up."

"Great," Mark said, matching her false lightness. "Claire is still thinking Thai food for lunch. We're starving."

"Sounds perfect," Emily replied, stepping past him into the house, her mind already calculating how to navigate the precarious path ahead.

9

THE BREAKING POINT

Three days had passed since Emily's **revelation** about Sarah's true background. Three days of maintaining a facade of normalcy at home, of family dinners and casual conversations that felt like performances in a play in which only Emily knew the real script. Mark had been attentive, almost hovering, while maintaining a veneer of everyday domesticity that felt increasingly suffocating.

Detective Ramirez had confirmed parts of Sarah's

story—she had indeed been an investigative journalist in Chicago before abruptly leaving the *Tribune*. He'd also verified that Jeffrey Winters's death was being investigated as suspicious rather than suicide. But the web of connections and motivations remained murky, with Mark's role still undefined.

"We're making progress on the financial records," Ramirez had told her during their last call. "Just maintain normal routines while we build the case."

Normal routines. As if anything about their lives had remained normal.

Emily checked her watch as she walked through Parkside Plaza, a small shopping center four blocks from their home. The late-afternoon sun cast long shadows across the nearly empty parking lot. Mark had left the house an hour ago to pick up dessert for after dinner. Emily was relieved, at first, needing space from Mark's watchful presence and time to think. But her relief soon turned to suspicion as the time dragged on. It was a ten-minute errand. Where was he? She decided to drive over and see what the holdup was.

Claire was at debate team practice—the one routine Emily insisted they maintain despite Mark's subtle suggestions that perhaps Claire should stay home more often, "given everything that's happening." Emily had been adamant; their daughter deserved whatever normalcy they could preserve. She was glad she didn't need to explain to anyone why she was heading over to the bakery instead of simply calling him. She had a sneaking suspicion he had taken a little detour.

As she passed the small alley between the bakery and the dry cleaners, raised voices caught her attention. Angry, urgent voices that seemed oddly familiar. Emily slowed, her instincts suddenly alert.

"You've compromised everything," a man hissed—Tom Mitchell's voice, unmistakable after she'd heard it at Onyx Coffee. "The whole operation is at risk because you couldn't control your wife."

Emily froze, then carefully edged closer to the alley entrance, positioning herself behind a large planter, where she could hear without being seen.

"I've handled it," Mark's voice replied, tight with tension. "Emily doesn't know anything concrete."

"She went to the police!" Tom's voice rose dangerously. "She's been seen with that reporter. Don't tell me that's 'handled.'"

Reporter. Sarah. So Mark knew about Sarah's background.

"Lower your voice," a third man said—someone Emily didn't recognize. His tone carried authority, a cold command that immediately silenced the others. "This public argument is exactly the kind of attention we don't need."

Emily risked a glance around the planter. Three men

stood in the shadowed alley—Tom, Mark, and a silver-haired man she recognized from the coffee shop meeting. The older man wore an expensive suit, his posture radiating confidence and control.

"The situation requires immediate resolution," the silver-haired man continued. "Johnson, you assured us your wife was contained. You're either incompetent or compromised."

"I'm neither," Mark insisted, his voice hardening. "But extreme measures aren't necessary. Emily trusts me. I've redirected her suspicions toward Tom—"

"You did what?" Tom interrupted, his face contorting with fury.

"—and she's backed off. The investigation will hit a dead end without her testimony."

The silver-haired man studied Mark with cold calculation. "Reynolds wants certainty, not assurances. The shipment next week is too valuable to risk."

"I need forty-eight hours," Mark pleaded, a desperation in his voice Emily had never heard before. "I'll get Emily and Claire out of town. A family emergency— my father's health. Once they're away from Ramirez, from that reporter—"

"That timeline is unacceptable," the silver-haired man cut him off. "Reynolds has authorized immediate containment protocols."

Tom smirked. "I told you he'd never make the hard

choice. He's too soft."

"This isn't about being soft," Mark snapped. "It's about unnecessary risk. Harm my family, and I have nothing left to lose. You think I wouldn't burn everything down? Every record, every account, every connection?"

The threat hung in the air, heavy with implication. Emily's breath caught in her throat. Was Mark threatening them to protect her and Claire? Or simply protecting himself from the consequences of his actions?

"Your insubordination is noted," the silver-haired man said coldly. "Perhaps Tom is right about your priorities."

"My priority has always been the operation," Mark insisted. "Fifteen years without incidents. Hundreds of millions processed. One problem doesn't erase that record."

The silver-haired man checked his watch. "You have twenty-four hours to resolve the situation with your wife. After that, we implement containment protocols with or without your cooperation."

"And what exactly does that mean?" Mark demanded.

"It means," Tom interjected with a cruel smile, "that if you won't handle your wife, we will. Along with anyone she's talked to."

Emily backed away silently, heart hammering against her ribs. They were talking about killing her. About killing Sarah, possibly Ramirez, too. And Mark was negotiating for time rather than rejecting the premise outright.

She'd heard enough. More than enough. Whatever

game Mark was playing, whatever his true motivations, the danger was immediate and lethal. She needed to grab Claire and get somewhere safe before Mark's twenty-four-hour window expired.

As she turned to hurry away, her foot caught on the edge of the planter, sending a small cascade of pebbles skittering across the pavement. The sound, insignificant in normal circumstances, echoed in the quiet plaza like gunshots.

The voices in the alley immediately fell silent.

Emily didn't wait to see if they'd investigate. She moved quickly toward the parking lot, maintaining a casual pace despite every instinct screaming at her to run. Her car was parked at the far end—too far. She fumbled for her keys, glancing over her shoulder.

Tom emerged from the alley first, scanning the plaza with narrowed eyes. When his gaze locked on her, recognition flashed across his features, followed by something much colder.

He said something to the others, still hidden in the alley shadows, and started walking purposefully in her direction.

Emily abandoned any pretense of casualness and ran. Her keys slipped from her trembling fingers, clattering to the pavement. No time to retrieve them. She changed course, heading for the busy street beyond the plaza.

"Emily!" Mark's voice called from behind her.

"Emily, wait!"

She didn't look back, focusing only on reaching the street where there would be witnesses, traffic, or safety in public visibility.

Heavy footsteps pounded behind her, gaining rapidly. A hand grabbed her arm, spinning her around roughly. Tom Mitchell's face, flushed with exertion and anger, loomed before her.

"Going somewhere, Mrs. Johnson?" he asked, his grip painfully tight on her upper arm.

"Let go of me," Emily demanded, her voice steadier than she felt. "People are watching."

"Actually, they're not," Tom replied with a cold smile. "Funny how people mind their own business in this town."

He was right. The few shoppers in the plaza were distant, absorbed in their own errands, oblivious to her predicament.

"Tom, let her go." Mark approached, his expression a complex mixture of anger and fear.

"She heard everything," Tom said, not loosening his grip. "This is exactly the situation Reynolds wanted to avoid."

"She's my wife," Mark insisted. "I'll handle this."

"Like you've handled everything else?" Tom scoffed.

The silver-haired man joined them, his calm demeanor somehow more frightening than Tom's obvious aggression. He studied Emily as one might examine an unexpected insect in an otherwise pristine home.

"Mrs. Johnson," he said, his voice cultured, almost pleasant. "An unfortunate circumstance."

"Let go of my wife, Tom," Mark repeated, an edge of desperation in his voice.

"Your wife has become a liability," the silver-haired man stated flatly. "One you promised to manage."

"And I will." Mark stepped closer, his eyes pleading with Emily. "Em, let me explain everything. Not here, but at home. Please."

Emily stared at her husband, seeing him clearly for perhaps the first time. Whatever his role in this operation, whatever his motivations, he was standing in a parking lot watching a man physically restrain his wife, and his response was to ask for a chance to "explain."

"Explain?" she repeated, disbelief coloring her voice. "I heard you discussing whether to kill me, Mark. Kill me and Claire."

"No," Mark shook his head vehemently. "Not Claire. Never Claire. I would never let that happen."

The fact that he didn't deny the threat against her specifically wasn't lost on Emily.

"Let her go," Mark told Tom again. "Now."

"This isn't your call," Tom replied.

"Actually," the silver-haired man interjected smoothly, "a public confrontation isn't in anyone's interest." He nodded to Tom, who reluctantly released

Emily's arm. "Mrs. Johnson, I suggest you accompany your husband home for a... family discussion."

The implied threat was clear. Emily rubbed her arm where Tom's fingers had dug in, already feeling bruises forming beneath her sleeve.

"My daughter gets out of debate practice in thirty minutes," she said, her mind racing for some advantage, some escape route. "If I'm not there to pick her up, she'll call the police."

It was a lie—Claire had arranged to go to a friend's house after practice—but Emily needed them to believe she had some form of protection, some insurance.

Mark seized on this. "I need to take Emily to get Claire. We'll go home and sort everything out privately."

The silver-haired man considered this, then nodded. "Very well. You have until 10 a.m. tomorrow. After that, containment protocols will proceed with or without your participation." He turned to Emily, his expression chilling. "Your daughter is a lovely girl, Mrs. Johnson. It would be a shame if her future were... disrupted."

The threat against Claire, delivered with such casual cruelty, triggered something primal in Emily. Rage surged through her, momentarily overpowering fear.

"If anything happens to my daughter," she said, her voice low and dangerous, "no contingency plan, no containment protocol will protect you. I will spend the rest of my life making sure you pay for it."

Surprise flickered briefly across the man's features before his composure returned. "Spirited. I can see why Mark has struggled to manage you." He turned to Mark. "Ten a.m. Do not disappoint us again."

He and Tom walked away, leaving Emily alone with Mark in the gathering twilight. The moment they were out of earshot, Mark reached for her.

"Emily—"

She recoiled from his touch. "Don't. Don't you dare touch me."

"You don't understand what's happening," Mark pleaded. "I've been trying to protect you and Claire—"

"By negotiating a timeline for my murder?" Emily hissed, fury and betrayal burning through her veins. "I heard you, Mark. I heard everything."

"It's not what you think." He glanced nervously in the direction Tom and the silver-haired man had gone. "We can't talk here. It's not safe."

"Nowhere is safe," Emily realized aloud. "Not with you."

"Please," Mark's voice cracked. "Let me take you home. Let me explain. If you run now, they'll implement containment immediately. Claire will be unprotected."

The mention of Claire pierced through Emily's anger. Whatever Mark had done, whatever he was involved in, Claire was still at her friend's house, unaware of the danger, vulnerable.

"My keys," she said numbly, pointing to where they'd fallen.

Mark retrieved them, then held out his hand. After a moment's hesitation, Emily took them, careful to avoid touching his fingers.

"Follow me home," Mark instructed. "Both our cars. I'll explain everything there, I promise."

Emily nodded mechanically, her mind already racing ahead. She needed to get to Claire, to get them both somewhere safe before Mark's deadline expired. But first, she needed information; she needed to understand exactly what she was dealing with and whom she could trust.

The drive home passed in a blur of automatic functions—turn signal, brake, accelerate—while her thoughts tumbled over one another in frantic disarray. Mark's car remained visible in her rearview mirror the entire time, a silent escort ensuring she didn't deviate from the expected route.

Their house looked exactly as she'd left it earlier— warm lights glowing in the gathering dusk, the porch light welcoming, the curtains drawn against the night.

Mark parked behind her, following her to the front door. Inside, the familiar surroundings felt alien, tainted by new knowledge. The family photos on the wall, the comfortable furniture, the children's artwork carefully framed—all of it now seemed like elaborate props in a production designed to conceal the truth.

"I need to call Claire," Emily said, her voice sounding distant to her own ears.

Mark nodded. "Of course. But Emily, before you do anything, you need to understand the situation."

She turned to face him fully, studying this stranger she'd married, this man who had fathered her child and shared her bed for fifteen years. "Explain, then. Explain why your business associates are planning to kill me. Explain why you're negotiating for time rather than rejecting the idea outright."

Mark sank onto the couch, suddenly looking older than his years. "It's complicated."

"Uncomplicate it," Emily demanded. "Because in less than twenty-four hours, according to that silver-haired man, I'm scheduled for 'containment.' So speak quickly."

"Reynolds isn't someone you can say no to," Mark began, his voice low. "Not directly. Not ever. I've been trying to find a way out for months, but each time I think I've found an exit, the noose tightens."

"Reynolds—the man using my maiden name as a code for his criminal operations?"

Mark nodded. "Jonathan Reynolds. He approached me fifteen years ago with an investment opportunity that seemed legitimate, profitable. By the time I realized what I'd gotten into, it was too late to walk away."

"Money laundering," Emily stated flatly.

"Among other things. Import-export schemes,

offshore accounts, shell companies. Reynolds has fingers in dozens of operations across the country. Tom oversees this region."

"And your role?"

Mark's expression was pained. "Financial management. Legitimate businesses investing in less legitimate operations, with profits cycling back through clean channels. It started small, just a few accounts. Then it grew."

"For fifteen years," Emily said, the full weight of the deception crashing down on her. "Our entire marriage."

"I tried to keep it separate from our life together," Mark insisted. "To protect you and Claire from knowing, from being implicated."

"Until I started noticing discrepancies," Emily concluded bitterly. "Until I found evidence you couldn't explain away."

Mark nodded miserably. "When you found the storage unit, when you went to the police—Reynolds sees you as a threat that needs to be eliminated. I've been trying to convince him you're contained, that you don't have enough evidence to pose a real danger."

"So you're negotiating for my life." Emily's voice was flat. "How generous."

"I'm trying to find a way out for all of us," Mark countered, a flash of anger breaking through his carefully controlled facade. "Do you think I want this? Do you think

I haven't spent years looking for an escape that doesn't end with us in witness protection or worse?"

"What I think," Emily said slowly, "is that you've had fifteen years to make different choices. Fifteen years to come clean, to find a way out that didn't involve criminal conspiracies and threats against your family. Instead, you chose this, over and over again, every single day."

Mark flinched as though she'd struck him. "It wasn't that simple."

"It never is," Emily agreed, surprising herself with the cold clarity of her thoughts. "But here we are—you've negotiated until 10 a.m. tomorrow before your associates implement 'containment protocols.' So what's your plan, Mark? How do you intend to save your family in the next fourteen hours?"

"We need to leave town," Mark said immediately. "Tonight. I've been preparing for this possibility—there's money, new identities, a place they won't find us."

"Running," Emily translated. "Uprooting Claire from her home, her school, her friends. Becoming fugitives."

"Being alive," Mark corrected sharply. "Reynolds doesn't make empty threats, Emily. If we're still here tomorrow morning, you'll disappear. They'll make it look like an accident, or a robbery gone wrong, or a random act of violence. And I'll be expected to grieve publicly while continuing to process their money, with the understanding that Claire's safety depends on my cooperation."

The calculated cruelty of the scenario turned Emily's blood cold. "And if we run? How long before they find us? How many years do we spend looking over our shoulders, waiting for them to catch up?"

"I have leverage," Mark insisted. "Information on their operations, account details, connections Reynolds wouldn't want exposed. It's insurance—enough to keep them from hunting us too aggressively."

"The storage unit," Emily realized. "That's what those documents really were. Insurance against Reynolds."

Mark nodded. "Everything I've done—the secret accounts, the storage unit, the coded records—it's all been preparation for this moment. A way out when it became necessary."

Emily studied her husband, weighing his words against his actions. "Why should I believe you? You've lied to me for fifteen years. You've manipulated evidence, gaslit me when I found the truth, and worked with people who casually discuss murder as a business solution."

"Because despite everything, I love you and Claire," Mark said, his voice breaking. "Whatever you think of me, whatever I've done, that has never been a lie."

The declaration hung in the air between them, a plea for understanding and forgiveness, for one last chance.

Emily thought of Claire, innocent and unaware, currently laughing with friends, doing homework, living a normal teenage life that could be shattered in an instant. She thought of Sarah, whose investigation had placed her directly in Reynolds's crosshairs. She thought of Detective Ramirez, who might also be targeted for "containment" if Reynolds felt threatened.

"I need to call Claire," Emily said again, her decision crystallizing. "And then I need to make another call."

Mark's expression tightened with alarm. "Who? Emily, you can't involve anyone else. It puts them at risk."

"You've already put everyone I care about at risk," she replied coldly. "Now I need to try to save them."

She pulled out her phone and dialed Claire's number, stepping away from Mark, maintaining enough distance that he couldn't interfere if she said something he didn't like.

Claire answered on the third ring, her voice bright with teenage enthusiasm. "Mom! Jenna's mom said I can sleep over if it's okay with you. We're working on our history project, and it's actually going really well for once."

The normality of the request, the ordinary teenage concerns, created such cognitive dissonance against the backdrop of death threats and escape plans that Emily nearly broke down. But she kept her voice steady.

"That sounds great, honey. Let me talk to Jenna's mom for a minute, okay?"

After confirming the sleepover arrangements with Jenna's mother—a woman Emily had known for years through PTA meetings and school functions—she ended the call with a forced cheerfulness that felt like glass in her throat.

"Claire's staying at Jenna's tonight," she told Mark, watching his reaction carefully.

Relief and worry battled across his features. "Good. That gives us time to pack and make arrangements." He hesitated. "Who else were you planning to call?"

Emily held his gaze steadily. "Sarah."

Mark's face darkened. "Absolutely not. She's part of the problem—her investigation, her recordings of Tom. She's on their radar already."

"Which is exactly why she needs to be warned," Emily countered. "Reynolds threatened anyone I've talked to. That includes Sarah and Detective Ramirez."

"Calling them now just creates more complications," Mark argued. "We need to focus on getting ourselves to safety first."

"No," Emily said firmly. "I'm not leaving them exposed to 'containment protocols' without warning. Not happening."

Mark ran a hand through his hair, frustration evident in every line of his body. "Emily, please. There isn't time—"

"Make time," she cut him off. "Because I'm not going anywhere with you until I've warned them. And if you try to force me, I'll scream so loudly the neighbors call the police, and neither of us gets out before Reynolds's deadline."

They locked eyes in a silent battle of wills. After a moment, Mark looked away first.

"Fine. Make your calls. But be careful what you say. Phone lines might be monitored."

Emily nodded, already dialing Sarah's number. It went straight to voicemail—unusual for Sarah, who typically answered promptly.

"Sarah, it's Emily. Call me as soon as you get this. It's urgent." She kept the message deliberately vague, heeding Mark's warning about monitoring.

Next, she tried Ramirez, with the same result—straight to voicemail. A cold feeling settled in her stomach. Could Reynolds have already implemented "containment" for the others while focusing on Mark's deadline for Emily?

"No answer from either of them," she told Mark, unable to keep the worry from her voice. "They both told me to call if I needed them. Why aren't they answering?"

"We need to go," Mark urged. "Now. While we still can."

Emily hesitated, torn between the need to ensure Sarah and Ramirez were safe and the urgency of protecting herself and Claire.

The decision was made for her when the doorbell rang, the sound jarring in the tense atmosphere. Mark froze, then moved toward the entryway window to peek outside.

"Who is it?" Emily whispered, suddenly fearful that

Reynolds had decided not to wait until morning after all.

Mark's expression shifted from tension to confusion. "It's Lisa Turner."

Lisa. The kindergarten teacher neighbor who'd been at the coffee shop with Tom. Who Mark claimed was helping him track suspicious transactions, but who Sarah had never connected to her investigation.

"Don't answer it," Emily said immediately.

"If we don't, it looks suspicious," Mark countered. "She can see the lights are on, she knows we're home."

The doorbell rang again, more insistent this time.

"Emily?" Lisa's voice called through the door. "I know you're home. We need to talk. It's important."

Emily and Mark exchanged a look of silent communication—the kind that develops between couples over years of shared life, regardless of secrets or betrayals. Mark nodded slightly, understanding her unspoken question, and moved toward the kitchen.

"One minute, Lisa!" Emily called, her voice convincingly normal despite her racing heart.

She waited until Mark had retrieved what she needed from the kitchen drawer before approaching the door. The weight of the object in her hand provided a grim reassurance as she unlocked the deadbolt.

Lisa stood on the porch, her usual neighborly smile replaced by a tense, urgent expression. "Emily, thank god. I've been trying to reach you—" She stopped abruptly, noticing Mark hovering in the background. "Mark. You're home early."

"Work wrapped up sooner than expected," he replied smoothly. "What brings you by, Lisa?"

Lisa hesitated, clearly uncomfortable with Mark's presence. "I... actually needed to talk to Emily. About the, um, book club selections."

"We don't have a book club, Lisa," Emily said quietly, her hand tightening around the object concealed behind her back. "Why don't you tell us why you're really here?"

Lisa's gaze darted between them, calculation evident in her expression. After a moment, her demeanor changed, the pretense of a friendly neighbor dropping away entirely.

"Reynolds sent me," she said simply. "There's been a change of plans."

Mark stepped forward, positioning himself slightly in front of Emily. "What kind of change?"

"Containment protocols have been accelerated. The timeline is compromised." Lisa's eyes fixed on Emily. "Tom believes your wife contacted authorities after your... discussion in the plaza parking lot."

"I haven't called anyone," Emily lied smoothly. "Check my phone records."

"Nevertheless, Reynolds is unwilling to wait until morning." Lisa reached into her purse, causing both Emily and Mark to tense. She withdrew an envelope. "These are new instructions. You're to proceed to the cabin immediately. Both of you."

The cabin. Emily remembered Mark cutting off his colleague Jeff when he'd mentioned "the cabin weekend" at the holiday party. Another piece of the puzzle clicking into place.

Mark took the envelope, his expression carefully neutral. "What about Claire?"

"Claire is being collected from her friend's house as we speak," Lisa stated, as casually as if discussing a carpool arrangement. "She'll join you at the cabin tomorrow, after everything is... settled."

Ice flooded Emily's veins. They were taking Claire. Using her daughter as leverage to ensure compliance.

"No," Emily said, the single syllable sharp as a blade. "Absolutely not."

Lisa's expression hardened. "This isn't a negotiation, Emily. Reynolds has made his decision. Mark knows the consequences of defiance."

"Tell Reynolds he can go to hell," Emily snarled, revealing the kitchen knife she'd been concealing behind her back. "My daughter stays out of this."

Lisa didn't flinch at the sight of the weapon. Instead, she smiled coldly. "Always the fighter. I told Tom you wouldn't go quietly." She reached back into her purse. "Unfortunately, we prepared for that possibility."

The gun that appeared in Lisa's hand looked almost toylike—small, discreet, but unmistakably real. "Now, let's try this again. You will both proceed to the cabin immediately. Claire will be brought there tomorrow. Any deviation from these instructions will have severe consequences for all three of you."

Emily felt Mark tense beside her, ready to lunge at Lisa despite the weapon trained on them. She placed a restraining hand on his arm. A physical confrontation would end badly—even if they overpowered Lisa, Reynolds would know they'd gone off-script. Claire would pay the price.

"Fine," Emily said, lowering the knife. "We'll go to the cabin. But I want proof Claire is safe, or the deal's off."

Lisa considered this, then nodded. "Once we're on the road, you'll receive confirmation. Now put down the knife, gather what you need, and let's go. Reynolds is not a patient man."

Emily placed the knife on the entryway table, her mind racing through scenarios, seeking some way out of this trap. Mark moved closer, his presence both reassuring and infuriating—he had brought this danger into their lives, yet he was the only other person who understood exactly what was at stake.

"Fifteen minutes," Lisa instructed. "Pack only essentials. I'll be watching from here."

As they moved toward the stairs, Mark's hand found Emily's, squeezing gently. She didn't pull away—not because she'd forgiven him, but because in this moment of crisis, they needed to present a united front. For Claire's sake, if nothing else.

"The cabin is isolated," Mark whispered as they entered their bedroom. "But my insurance documents aren't at the storage unit anymore. They're hidden where only I can access them."

Emily began gathering clothes mechanically, her voice equally low. "What are they planning for us at this cabin?"

Mark's expression was grim. "Nothing good. Reynolds doesn't leave loose ends."

"We're not going to the cabin," Emily decided, throwing essentials into a small bag. "We're going to get Claire first."

"They'll expect that," Mark warned. "They'll be watching Jenna's house."

"Then we need help." Emily pulled out her phone again, trying Sarah and Ramirez once more. Still no answer from either. "There has to be someone we can trust."

Mark hesitated, then reached into his wallet and extracted a small card hidden behind his driver's license. "There might be. But it's a risk."

Emily examined the card—a name and phone number, nothing else. "Who is this?"

"Someone who's been trying to build a case against Reynolds for years. Someone who approached me six months ago when they suspected Preston Financial was involved in money laundering."

Understanding dawned. "A federal agent?"

Mark nodded. "I've been feeding them information. Not enough to implicate myself directly, but enough to help their investigation. It's part of my insurance policy—cooperation in exchange for immunity when it all comes apart."

Emily stared at her husband, reassessing him yet again. "So you've been what—a reluctant informant? Playing both sides?"

"Trying to find a way out that doesn't end with us dead or in prison," Mark corrected. "Call it self-preservation if you want, but everything I've done has been to protect our family."

The revelation added another layer to Mark's complex motivations—not simply a criminal seeking to avoid consequences, but perhaps a man trapped in a situation he couldn't escape, making desperate choices to protect what mattered most.

"Ten minutes!" Lisa called up the stairs.

Emily handed him the card back. "We'll call your contact once we're clear of Lisa. But Mark—" she fixed him with an unwavering stare, "—if this is another manipulation, if Claire is harmed in any way because of your choices, there will be nowhere on earth you can hide from me."

Mark held her gaze, something like respect flickering in his eyes. "Understood."

They finished packing in tense silence, both acutely aware of Lisa waiting below, of Claire in potential danger, of Reynolds and his "containment protocols" closing in around them.

While they descended the stairs with their hastily packed bags, Emily felt a strange calm settling over her. The weeks of uncertainty, of questioning her own perceptions, of trying to determine who was lying and who could be trusted—all of that had crystallized into a single, clear priority: Protect Claire at all costs.

Whatever happened next, whatever revelations or betrayals awaited, Emily had reached her breaking point. No more passive investigation, no more waiting for others to make moves. From this moment forward, she would take control of her family's fate, with or without Mark's help, regardless of the danger.

Lisa gestured toward the door with her gun, a cold smile playing at her lips. "After you."

Emily stepped outside into the cool night air, Mark close behind her. The peaceful suburban street looked exactly as it always had—porch lights glowing, sprinklers hissing on manicured lawns, the distant sound of a dog barking—all oblivious to the life-and-death drama unfolding in their midst.

As Lisa directed them toward her car, Emily caught Mark's eye, a silent understanding passing between them. Whatever their past, whatever secrets and lies had built the foundation of their marriage, they now faced a common enemy and shared a single purpose.

For the next few hours, until they could ensure Claire's safety, they would be partners in this dangerous game. What came after—reconciliation, separation, legal consequences—all of that would have to wait.

The only thing that mattered now was surviving the night and saving their daughter from Reynolds' "containment protocols," whatever it took.

10

SHATTERED ILLUSIONS

Lisa's sedan cut through the darkness, headlights illuminating the winding road that led away from the suburbs toward the mountains. Emily sat rigid in the passenger seat, mind racing through escape scenarios, each more desperate than the last. Mark occupied the back seat, Lisa having insisted on this arrangement "to avoid any collaborative heroics."

"How much farther to this cabin?" Emily asked, breaking the tense silence.

"About forty minutes," Lisa replied without taking her

eyes off the road. "Reynolds prefers isolation for sensitive conversations."

Emily glanced at her watch: 9:17 p.m. Claire would be settling in at Jenna's house, unaware that strangers intended to "collect" her. The thought made Emily's blood boil with protective fury.

"And where exactly is my daughter right now?" she demanded.

Lisa's lips curved in a cold smile. "Being monitored. The specifics aren't your concern."

"Like hell they aren't," Emily snapped. "I want proof she's safe, or this car isn't going another mile."

Lisa laughed. "And how exactly do you plan to stop it?"

From the back seat, Mark spoke for the first time since they'd left the house. "Emily, antagonizing Lisa won't help Claire."

The rational part of Emily knew he was right, but every maternal instinct screamed against this passive compliance while Claire was in danger. She caught Mark's eye in the rearview mirror, trying to gauge if he had a plan beyond following Reynolds's orders. His expression revealed nothing, though his hand moved subtly toward his pocket, where Emily knew he kept the federal agent's contact information.

Lisa's phone rang, breaking the tension. "Yes?" she answered crisply. "Understood. We're approximately forty minutes out... No, no complications... Of course." She disconnected and glanced at Emily. "Your daughter sends her regards."

Emily's heart nearly stopped. "What does that mean? You said she was still at Jenna's."

"Plans change," Lisa replied smoothly. "Reynolds thought it best to accelerate the timeline."

"If you've hurt her—" Emily began.

"Relax," Lisa cut her off. "Claire is perfectly fine. She's simply been relocated to ensure your continued cooperation."

Mark leaned forward, his voice deadly calm. "Lisa—"

Lisa rolled her eyes. "Save the threats, Mark. They don't suit you. Besides, Claire's safety depends entirely on your behavior at the cabin."

Emily's mind processed this new information with cold clarity. They had Claire. The stakes had just escalated beyond anything she'd imagined. Yet, strangely, the confirmation brought focus rather than panic. With Claire directly involved, failure wasn't an option.

She needed to contact help, but her phone had been confiscated before they left the house. Mark still had his— she'd seen Lisa overlook it during her cursory search. Somehow, she needed to create an opportunity for him to make that call.

"I need to use the bathroom," she announced abruptly.

Lisa sighed with irritation. "Can't it wait?"

"Not unless you want me to soil your car," Emily replied bluntly. "There's a gas station coming up on the right. Two minutes, that's all I need."

Lisa hesitated, then relented with obvious annoyance. "Fine. Two minutes. But Mark stays in the car with me."

As Lisa pulled into the gas station, Emily noted it was nearly deserted—only one other vehicle, parked at the far end of the lot. Less than ideal for creating a scene that might attract attention, but it would have to do.

"I'm watching the door," Lisa warned as Emily exited the car. "Don't try anything stupid."

Emily nodded, walking deliberately toward the convenience store. The moment she was inside, out of Lisa's direct line of sight, she moved with urgent purpose toward the clerk—a bored-looking young man scrolling on his phone.

"I need help," she said in a low, urgent voice. "The woman in that car outside has a gun. She's kidnapped me and my husband, and they have our daughter."

The clerk looked up with wide eyes, clearly trying to determine if this was a prank. "Lady, are you serious?"

"Deadly serious," Emily replied, glancing nervously toward the door. "Call 911. Tell them we're being taken to a cabin in the mountains, specifically—"

The bell above the door jingled as Lisa entered, her expression pleasant but her eyes cold as ice. "Everything okay in here, Emily? You're taking longer than expected."

The clerk looked between them, uncertainty written across his face.

"Just picking up some aspirin," Emily improvised smoothly, grabbing a bottle from the nearby shelf. "Stress headache."

Lisa's smile didn't reach her eyes. "Understandable. Let's not keep Reynolds waiting, though."

Emily approached the counter, placing the aspirin down along with a five-dollar bill. As the clerk made change, she locked eyes with him, silently pleading for him to understand the danger. He gave an almost imperceptible nod as he handed her the receipt—a small note scribbled on the back: "CALLING."

Relief flooded through her. Someone knew they were in trouble. It might not be enough, but it was something.

Back in the car, Lisa's phone rang again. She answered, listened briefly, then handed it to Mark in the back seat. "Reynolds wants a word."

Mark took the phone cautiously. "Yes?" His face drained of color as he listened. "I understand... Yes, she's right here... No, no complications..." He handed the phone to Emily, his expression grim. "He wants to speak with you."

Emily took the phone, her hand steady despite her racing heart. "Hello?"

"Mrs. Johnson." The cultured voice of the silver-haired man from the plaza sent chills down her spine. "I hope you're enjoying the drive. The mountains are beautiful this time of year."

"Where is my daughter?" Emily demanded, dispensing with pleasantries.

"Ah, direct. I appreciate that quality." Reynolds sounded almost amused. "Claire is comfortable, I assure you. Currently enjoying hot chocolate and marshmallows at my private residence, completely unaware of the precarious situation her parents have created."

"Let her go," Emily said. "She doesn't know anything about any of this."

"Of course she doesn't," Reynolds agreed reasonably. "Which is why she remains unharmed. Her continued well-being depends entirely on your cooperation when you arrive at the cabin. Specifically, your willingness to sign certain documents transferring control of your assets to a management company of my choosing."

The pieces clicked into place. This wasn't just about silencing her—Reynolds wanted to use her and Mark as puppets, controlling their finances, likely laundering money through their accounts with their forced cooperation.

"And if I refuse?" she asked, already knowing the answer.

"Then Claire becomes an orphan with a tragic story about her parents' murder-suicide following the discovery of her father's embezzlement." The coldness with which he delivered this threat made it all the more terrifying. "Your choice, Mrs. Johnson. Cooperation and life, or defiance and... Well, you understand the alternatives."

The line went dead. Emily handed the phone back to Lisa, her mind working furiously. Reynolds wanted them alive—at least initially—to sign documents, to establish his control. That gave them time, however limited.

She caught Mark's eye in the rearview mirror again, trying to communicate silently. He gave an almost imperceptible nod, his hand slipping into his pocket. The federal contact. He was going to make the call.

"I need to use the restroom, too," Mark announced suddenly. "That gas station was my last chance before the mountains."

Lisa's eyes narrowed. "Absolutely not. We're already behind schedule."

"Unless you want me to urinate in your car," Mark countered, "I suggest you pull over at the next opportunity."

Lisa cursed under her breath but began scanning for a suitable location. Two minutes later, she pulled onto a scenic overlook—a small parking area with a view of the valley below, completely deserted at this hour.

"Make it quick," she ordered, removing her gun from her purse and placing it openly on her lap as Mark exited the car.

Emily watched as Mark walked toward the guardrail, ostensibly to relieve himself with minimal privacy. In the dim illumination from the car's headlights, she could see him fumbling with something in his pocket—the phone, she hoped.

Lisa seemed distracted, checking her own phone for messages. Emily needed to create more time, more opportunity for Mark to make that critical call.

"I think I'm going to be sick," she announced abruptly, opening her door before Lisa could object.

"For God's sake," Lisa snapped, but Emily was already out of the car, staggering dramatically toward the opposite side of the overlook from Mark.

She leaned against the guardrail, making retching sounds while surreptitiously watching Mark. He had his phone out now, typing quickly, head bowed to shield the screen's glow. She needed to buy him more time.

"Lisa," she called weakly. "I think I need some water..."

Lisa emerged from the car, gun now concealed but clearly still accessible in her jacket pocket. "This isn't a road trip with comfort stops, Emily. Get back in the car. Now."

"Just... give me a minute," Emily pleaded, slumping against the guardrail. From the corner of her eye, she saw Mark press his phone to his ear, speaking rapidly in a hushed voice. Just a few more seconds...

The crack of a gunshot shattered the night, the bullet pinging off the guardrail inches from Emily's hand. She jerked upright in shock.

"That was a warning," Lisa said coldly, gun now openly aimed at Emily. "The next one won't miss. Get in the car. Both of you."

Mark had shoved his phone back into his pocket at the sound of the gunshot, his call cut short. But had it been enough? Had he managed to communicate their location, their danger?

As they drove the final stretch toward the cabin, the atmosphere in the car was electric with tension. Lisa kept her gun visible on her lap, her patience clearly exhausted. Emily measured the passing minutes with mounting anxiety, wondering if help would arrive in time, if Claire was truly safe, if they were driving toward their execution.

The cabin materialized out of the darkness—a substantial structure of wood and stone, remote but luxurious—with a black SUV already parked outside. Light spilled from the windows, indicating others were waiting inside.

"End of the line," Lisa announced, pulling up beside the SUV. "Remember, your cooperation ensures Claire's safety. Any heroics, any deviation from the script, and Reynolds makes a very difficult phone call."

Inside, the cabin was warm and well-appointed—a mountain retreat that would have seemed inviting under any other circumstances. The silver-haired Reynolds stood by a stone fireplace, whiskey glass in hand, the picture of civilized menace. Tom Mitchell sat at a dining table covered with documents, wearing an expression of smug satisfaction.

"Mr. and Mrs. Johnson," Reynolds greeted them smoothly. "Thank you for joining us on such short notice. I trust the drive was uneventful?"

"Where's my daughter?" Emily demanded immediately.

"Safe," Reynolds replied. "And she'll remain that way, provided we conclude our business efficiently." He gestured toward the table. "Please, sit. We have documents to discuss."

The "documents" were transfer forms, power of attorney declarations, and banking authorizations—all designed to give Reynolds complete control over their finances and property. The plan became clear as Tom explained the terms: Mark would continue working at Preston Financial, processing transactions as directed. Emily would maintain their perfect suburban charade, playing the role of oblivious wife. Their accounts would be used to launder money, their respectability providing cover for Reynolds's operations. Any deviation would result in "unfortunate consequences" for Claire.

"And what guarantee do we have that you'll keep your end of the bargain?" Mark asked, stalling for time as he reviewed each document with deliberate slowness.

Reynolds smiled thinly. "My word, of course."

"Not good enough," Emily interjected. "I want to

speak to Claire. Now.”

Reynolds considered this, then nodded to Lisa, who produced a phone and dialed a number, putting it on speaker.

“Hello?” Claire’s voice, sleepy and confused, filled the room.

Emily’s heart clenched. “Claire, honey, it’s Mom. Are you okay?”

“Mom? Why are you calling so late? Is everything all right?”

“Everything’s fine, sweetheart,” Emily lied smoothly. “Dad and I had to take care of some unexpected business. We just wanted to check on you.”

“I’m at Jenna’s,” Claire said, confusion evident in her voice. “We were sleeping...”

Emily frowned, looking at Reynolds in confusion. Claire was still at Jenna’s? Not taken, as they’d claimed?

Reynolds took the phone. “Sorry for the late call, Claire. Your parents just wanted to make sure you were enjoying your sleepover. Goodnight now.” He ended the call, smiling at Emily’s evident surprise. “You didn’t really think we’d involve a child directly, did you? Much cleaner to let her remain exactly where she is—while monitoring the situation, of course.”

“You lied,” Emily said, anger replacing fear.

“A necessary motivation,” Reynolds replied unapologetically. “You needed to understand the stakes.”

He pushed the stack of documents toward them. "Now, shall we proceed? The signature pages are flagged."

Emily exchanged a glance with Mark, a silent communication passing between them. Claire was safe—for now. But once they signed these papers, they would be irreversibly bound to Reynolds's operation, complicit in his crimes, and forever under his control.

Mark picked up a pen, hovering it over the first signature line. "And if we refuse?"

"Then this pleasant cabin becomes the site of a tragic murder-suicide," Reynolds said simply. "After which, as the legal guardian specified in your will, your brother Michael takes custody of Claire—who, I should mention, will be under our observation for the rest of her life. Insurance, you understand."

Emily felt sick. They had investigated so thoroughly, planned for every contingency. Even if she and Mark died here, Claire would never truly be free.

"Sign the papers, Mark," she said quietly. "We don't have a choice."

Mark looked at her, surprise evident in his expression. She held his gaze steadily, hoping he could read the message in her eyes. *Buy time. Help is coming. I hope.*

He nodded almost imperceptibly and began signing, taking his time with each document, asking clarifying questions, requesting time to read fine print. Emily followed suit, employing similar delaying tactics while surreptitiously checking her watch. How long since Mark's interrupted phone call? Would help arrive in time, or were they truly on their own?

As they worked through the stack of documents, a subtle shift occurred in the atmosphere. Lisa moved to the window, peering out into the darkness with growing tension. She whispered something to Reynolds, whose expression hardened.

"Accelerate the process," he instructed Tom. "We're concluding our business immediately."

Tom pushed the remaining documents forward aggressively. "No more stalling. Sign them. Now."

"Is something wrong?" Mark asked innocently, though Emily could see the hope kindling in his eyes.

"Nothing that concerns you," Reynolds replied coldly. "Sign the papers, or we move to the alternative conclusion."

Before either could respond, the cabin's lights suddenly went out, plunging them into darkness broken only by the fireplace's glow. Lisa cursed, moving away from the window with her gun drawn.

"Perimeter breach," she reported tersely. "Multiple figures approaching from the tree line."

"Federal agents!" a voice boomed from outside, amplified by a megaphone. "The cabin is surrounded. Come out with your hands up!"

Chaos erupted in an instant. Tom lunged for a briefcase, Reynolds moved toward what appeared to be a concealed back exit, and Lisa aimed her gun directly at Emily.

"No one's taking me in," she snarled, finger tightening on the trigger.

Mark launched himself across the table, tackling Lisa as the gun discharged. The bullet splintered wood inches from Emily's head. She dropped to the floor as more shots rang out. The FBI breached the front door, and Lisa returned fire from her position behind an overturned sofa.

"Emily!" Mark called from somewhere in the darkness. "Get down!"

She crawled toward his voice, her heart pounding as gunfire continued to exchange around her. The front door burst open, tactical lights cutting through the darkness, illuminating federal agents in bulletproof vests swarming into the cabin.

"Federal agents! Weapons down! On the ground, now!"

Reynolds made a dash for the back exit but was intercepted by agents coming in from all sides. Tom, attempting to destroy documents by tossing them into the fireplace, was tackled and handcuffed. Lisa, however, continued firing from her position, refusing to surrender.

"Emily," Mark's voice came again, closer now, strained with pain. "Over here."

She found him slumped against the wall near the overturned sofa, his hand pressed to his shoulder, blood seeping between his fingers. "You're hurt," she gasped.

"It's nothing," he grimaced. "Listen to me—Reynolds has a dead man's switch. If he doesn't check in every twelve hours, evidence of my involvement gets sent to the authorities. I need to talk to the agent in charge, explain the situation."

Emily stared at him, processing this new information. Even now, facing arrest, Mark was still calculating angles, still looking for a way to protect himself.

A final exchange of gunfire drew their attention. Lisa had made a break for the door and had been cut down by multiple agents. Her body lay still on the cabin floor, the threat she posed permanently neutralized.

As the chaos subsided, agents secured the scene, checking for survivors, collecting evidence. A woman in a tactical vest approached Mark and Emily, her badge identifying her as Special Agent Carmichael.

"Mr. and Mrs. Johnson?" she asked, kneeling beside them. "Are you injured?"

"He needs medical attention," Emily said, indicating Mark's shoulder. "Gunshot wound."

"Medics are on their way," Agent Carmichael assured them. "We received a partial distress call naming this location—just enough information to mobilize a response team. Was that you?"

Mark nodded weakly. "I've been feeding information to Agent Torres for months. Building a case against

Reynolds."

Agent Carmichael's expression revealed nothing. "We'll discuss that at headquarters. For now, let's get you both medical attention and protective custody."

As paramedics attended to Mark, Emily felt the adrenaline draining from her system, leaving bone-deep exhaustion in its wake. Reynolds and Tom were being led out in handcuffs, their empire crumbling around them. Lisa lay dead, her betrayal ending in the ultimate price.

"Claire," she remembered suddenly. "My daughter—"

"Agents are already at the location where she's staying," Carmichael assured her. "She's under protection and will remain so until we've accounted for all members of Reynolds's organization."

Emily nodded gratefully, allowing herself to be led outside to a waiting ambulance. The night air was cold and clear, stars visible above the mountain peaks. Whatever came next—Mark's potential prosecution, the dismantling of the money-laundering operation, the long process of rebuilding their lives—at least Claire was safe. At least the immediate danger had passed.

Detective Ramirez arrived a few minutes later, with three police cruisers. He made a beeline straight for Emily and apologized profusely for missing her call earlier. "When I tried to call back and you didn't answer, I knew something was wrong. We've been out looking for you since."

While medics checked her for injuries, Emily watched Mark being loaded into another ambulance, his expression unreadable in the flashing emergency lights. Had he truly been working with the FBI all along, trying to build an exit strategy? Or was this final claim just another manipulation, another attempt to save himself from the consequences of his actions?

She didn't know. Perhaps she never would. But she had survived, Claire was safe, and Reynolds's operation was exposed. For tonight, that would have to be enough.

The ambulance doors closed, and they began the descent from the mountain cabin, leaving behind the shattered illusions of her perfect suburban life. What lay ahead was uncertain, but for the first time in weeks, Emily felt something like hope flickering in the darkness—a small light guiding her toward whatever came next.

EPILOGUE

Three Months Later

The courthouse steps gleamed in the spring sunshine as Emily emerged from the final day of Reynolds's preliminary hearing. Her testimony had been exhaustive, detailing everything she had discovered about the money-laundering operation centered around Preston Financial.

Mark's fate remained uncertain. His claim of being a reluctant FBI informant had been partially corroborated by Agent Torres, though the extent of his cooperation—and whether it would be enough to mitigate his involvement in years of financial crimes—was still being determined by prosecutors. It was complicated, trying to untangle the different investigations that had been happening. Detective Ramirez was there, doing his best to support the case with his own findings.

Claire had weathered the storm with remarkable resilience, though the therapy sessions twice weekly suggested deeper wounds that would take time to heal. The revelation that her father had been living a double life, and that their comfortable existence had been built on criminal enterprise, had shaken her foundation. But she was strong—stronger than Emily had realized.

"Mrs. Johnson."

Emily turned to find Sarah waiting at the bottom of the courthouse steps, looking professional in a tailored blazer, press badge visible on a lanyard around her neck. Their relationship remained complicated—trust shattered, then partially rebuilt as Sarah's claims about her journalistic investigation had been verified.

"The Chicago *Tribune* is very interested in your exclusive story," Sarah said, falling into step beside Emily as they walked toward the parking lot. "Whenever you're ready to tell it."

"I'm not sure I'll ever be ready for that," Emily replied honestly. "Some parts of this might always be too painful to revisit."

Sarah nodded, understanding. "The offer stands. On or off the record, as a journalist, or as a friend."

Friend. The word hung between them, loaded with history and betrayal and the possibility of redemption.

"I'll think about it," Emily promised, reaching her car. "How's the Reynolds investigation coming? Any leads on the rest of his network?"

Sarah's expression turned serious. "That's actually why I wanted to catch you today. Something's emerged in my research that I thought you should know." She glanced around the parking lot, then lowered her voice. "Reynolds wasn't the top of the organization. He answered to someone else—someone whose name keeps appearing in offshore accounts, property records, shell companies."

Emily felt a chill despite the warm spring day. "Who?"

Sarah hesitated, then handed Emily a manila envelope.

"See for yourself. But be careful who you show this to. If I've found this connection, others might have as well."

Emily took the envelope but didn't open it. "Is Claire in danger?"

"I don't think so," Sarah assured her. "Not immediately. But information is protection in this situation. You should know what you're potentially dealing with."

With a final meaningful look, Sarah walked away, leaving Emily alone with the envelope. She sat in her car, staring at the seemingly innocuous paper folder that potentially contained yet another layer to the conspiracy that had nearly destroyed her family.

Part of her wanted to throw it away unopened, to focus solely on rebuilding her life with Claire and on healing their wounds and creating a new normal. But the larger part— the part that had refused to ignore inconsistencies, that had pursued the truth despite danger and betrayal—knew she couldn't walk away.

With steady hands, she opened the envelope and removed a single photograph. It showed Reynolds shaking hands with a distinguished-looking man at what appeared to be a charity gala. The man's face was instantly recognizable—a prominent political figure, currently campaigning for higher office.

Beneath the photo was a handwritten note in Sarah's distinctive script:

The real power behind Reynolds's operation. This

goes higher than anyone realizes. We've only scratched the surface.

Emily stared at the image, a new understanding dawning. The investigation hadn't ended with Reynolds's arrest. It had only just begun.

She started her car, carefully tucking the envelope into her purse. Claire was waiting at home, and for now, that remained Emily's priority—protecting her daughter and rebuilding their life together. But the truth still mattered. Justice still mattered.

And if Reynolds was merely a cog in a larger machine, perhaps her role in this story wasn't finished after all.

ABOUT THE AUTHOR

Chiara Robbins has always been fascinated by the quiet tension that hides behind everyday lives — the whispers, the questions, the things left unsaid. Behind Closed Doors is her debut novel, born from that curiosity and a love of twisty, character-driven stories that keep you turning the pages late into the night.

When she's not writing, Chiara enjoys people-watching in coffee shops, reading crime fiction, and wondering what secrets might be tucked behind the curtains of ordinary homes. She believes that the most powerful stories are the ones rooted in real emotions — fear, love, betrayal, and the strength to start over.

Chiara lives with her partner and an overly dramatic cat who insists on supervising every writing session. She's incredibly grateful to every reader who's taken a chance on a first-time author — and she hopes this is just the beginning.

You can connect with her at Chiara.Robbins.Author@gmail.com — she'd love to hear what you think.

ACKNOWLEDGMENTS

Writing Behind Closed Doors was one of those experiences that stretched me in all the best (and sometimes hardest) ways. It came with a fair share of doubt, rewrites, and those moments where I wondered if I'd ever get to the last page. But here we are — and I couldn't have done it alone.

To everyone who picked up this book — thank you. Truly. Whether you read it in one sitting or squeezed it into your busy days, I'm so grateful you spent time with Emily's story. I hope it made you feel something. I hope it made you think.

To my family and friends — thank you for your patience, for listening when I rambled about plot holes, and for cheering me on even when I was running on fumes. You kept me grounded when I got lost in the chaos of it all.

To the people who helped shape this book — from editing to design to advice I didn't even know I needed — thank you. Your care and expertise helped me tell this story the way it deserved to be told.

And finally, to anyone who's ever had that gut feeling that something wasn't right, who's asked hard questions, or stood up when it would've been easier to look away — this story is for you. Stay curious. Stay brave.

With love,

Chiara